WHAT S

Book 3

Crime, Commitment & Consequences

Patricia E. Gitt

Angela—
Thank you always.
Love, Pat

Print Edition ISBN 987-1-7345478-3-2

Ebook Edition ISBN 987-1-7345478-4-9

This book was printed in the United States

What She Didn't Know, Book 1 – Blinded by Love

Print Edition ISBN 987-1-7341584-9-6

Ebook Edition ISBN 987-7345478-0-1

What She Didn't Know 2 – Of Widowhood and Murder

Print Edition ISBN -978-1-7345478-1-8

Ebook Edition ISBN – 978-1-7345478-2-5

Published by Athena Book Publishing

New York, New York

Athenabookpublishing.com

Also, by Patricia E. Gitt

The New York Mystery Series

CEO

ASAP – as soon as possible – A Settling of Scores

TBD – to be determined – A Game Changer

FYI An Unintended Consequence

Website: patriciagitt.com

Dedication

I am eternally grateful to my parents, Connie and Mike Gitt, for many gifts. One in particular is by their example... Dreams can come true through hard work and perseverance.

"It's never too late to be what you might have been."
~ George Eliot

Contents

Prologue

Sally Compton Scott survived the murder investigation of a young reporter, Lisa Clark; a traumatic period in which Sally never knew if she would be the next victim.

Despite her financial worries and the painful loss of the love of her life, her husband, Tyler, Sally persevered.

Now with her accounting business humming, and a new man in her life, Sally's unbridled curiosity leads her into unexpected territory when she agrees to help the reporter's aunt Susan, finish writing Lisa Clark's explosive book on money laundering.

Will Sally's involvement once again put her in the crosshairs of these same criminals with a history of double-dealing that harken back to the Italian Mob of the Roaring Twenties? Sally ignores the detective's warnings not to get involved, believing that while the wheels of justice have stalled, she will be safe with the criminals in custody and awaiting trial.

Armed with a passion to complete Lisa's work, Sally and Susan begin their research. Will they uncover money laundering activities that go back generations, or something more sinister? Will their study of the people behind Lisa's murder reveal a complex criminal empire? Is this a local law and order situation, or international in scope?

Once again, Sally is faced with the challenge of uncovering what she didn't know.

Chapter 1

Sally Scott stood at the entrance of the small Catholic church, and as she looked down the central aisle toward the altar, felt a serenity that had been missing in her life. The midday sun streamed through the arched stained-glass windows high on the wall behind the altar, giving a spiritual glow to the stone-floored building. For the past half year, she'd been living with the anguish of having spotted a murdered woman in the elevator of her apartment building... someone she had never met... but who had become central to her everyday life.

It was midday in Manhattan, that time between Thanksgiving and Christmas, and the church was empty except for the few people in the front pews. All present were there for a private memorial service celebrating Lisa Clark's life. The young woman had been a reporter researching a story about a criminal enterprise and was murdered to keep her quiet.

Sally thought that there would be more family and friends in attendance, only now realizing how little she knew about the reporter. Having become personally involved in the murder investigation, she knew more about the murderer than the victim.

While Sally didn't know most of the half dozen or so people in attendance, she did recognize two of her accounting clients, Megan Riley, wearing black instead of one of her brightly colored pants suits, and Indigo, her usually stylish self in a dark gray knit dress that floated over her slim body. Megan regarded Lisa as a friend and customer of her dress shop, Fashionably Yours. And Indigo, owner of the bakery Southern Comfort, was there to support Sally, knowing that finding the killer had become her personal quest for the truth.

Walking down the main aisle, she slipped into the second row of pews behind Susan Clark, Lisa's aunt. Reaching out and giving her shoulder a light squeeze in greeting, she felt Susan's hand touching hers in response and then left the woman to her thoughts.

A queer feeling made Sally look to the balcony where she spotted a well-built man stuffed into a quilted jacket and wearing sunglasses, taking a seat in the last row. Not recognizing him, she turned her attention to the priest as he walked to the altar. Aged, with gray hair and wrinkled brow, he was a comforting sight. His quiet voice spoke of religious strength and tranquility.

As the priest bowed his head, Sally said a silent prayer for the dead woman, then looked over to the lace-covered table in front of the altar. The memorial display held tributes to the young woman they were there to honor, including a photograph mounted in a silver frame, a navy-blue ceramic urn, and a matching vase of lilies. Studying the photograph, Sally wondered if it had been taken by a friend. Instead of a staid professional pose, Lisa was seated at a desk supporting her head in her hand and wearing a smile of satisfaction. *Who wouldn't want to read anything this friendly person wrote?*

Leaning forward, Sally whispered, "Mrs. Clark, are we waiting for Lisa's parents?"

Shaking her head no, Sally heard her whisper they had passed away some time before. Apparently, Susan was the only family the young woman had. *How sad. Even as a widow, I'm blessed with a mother and family by marriage.*

Susan Clark rose after the first prayer and walking to a side lectern, stood with a straight back and composed expression, closed her eyes for a brief moment. Then, in a strong but soft voice began, "Friends, I would like to thank you for helping me honor my niece. She was an extraordinary young woman filled with passion for her work as an investigative reporter. In addition to being a kind, lovely person, she was smart, hardworking, and had many other gifts. One I found to be exceptional. It was her ability to read people. A talent too few today even bother to develop. Lisa used this talent to develop the business profiles she wrote for the newspaper. Instead of mourning her passing, I would like you to join me in celebrating her life. Thank you." Susan threw a kiss toward the urn containing her niece's ashes and, with head bowed, returned to her seat.

Sally watched as a short blonde woman fashionably dressed all in black, from shoes and stockings to tailored dress, stepped up to the lectern. "I'm Dina Wagner and was Lisa's editor. She arrived at the newspaper four years ago, shortly after earning her graduate degree in journalism. I remember her interview because, unlike others wanting a job, she had been filled with enthusiasm. When I asked her what kind of articles she hoped to work on, she said those that showcased the talent and success of hardworking people. She didn't care what they did. She told me that the world would always have problems, but she hoped to shine a light on successful people with a special talent and passion. After a brief trial period, understanding that I had a true investigative reporter and storyteller in my midst, I asked her to submit a list of ideas for future columns. That list featured small, unique businesses, not the larger emporiums familiar to most New Yorkers." Looking up, Dina smiled. "And with each profile, our circulation grew. Lisa didn't need an editor. She needed the freedom to follow her instincts. Goodbye, Lisa. You will be missed."

After the service, Susan Clark stood by the front door of the church, thanking those who had paid their respects. Sally watched the bone-thin Dina Wagner simply nod to Lisa's aunt as she left without offering a personal note of sympathy. Then a jean-clad youth, who looked like he was still in high school, reached up and gave Susan a hug. "Mrs. Clark, I'm Hank Washington, Lisa's photographer. She was my favorite," he gushed. "You know, when we first worked together, Lisa said she wanted her columns to reflect the person's enjoyment, not the problems associated with their business. She trusted me and said my photos were the highlight of her stories."

As Sally stood off to the side, she got that prickly feeling that she was being watched. Looking up to the balcony, she didn't see anything suspicious. *I'm just imagining things.* Shaking her head, she turned her focus on a full-figured young woman in a floral dress, clearly distraught with tears trickling down plump cheeks and a well-used tissue clasped in her hand. Sally thought the emotional young woman might have been a girlfriend. "Mrs. Clark, my name is Olivia Thompson and I loved your niece. She took me under her wing. Always made time to help me with a column. Being senior on the staff, she also helped me deal with Ms. Wagner's strict rules. I owe her so much. I'll never forget her." Reaching out, she hugged Susan and quickly turned and left the church.

After Indigo and Megan stopped by to pay their respects, Sally, not wanting Susan to be left alone with her grief, reached out to delay her departure. "Susan, why don't Megan, Indigo, and I take you to Indigo's tea shop? My treat. A personal chance to pay our respects."

"Oh, yes, Mrs. Clark. It's right around the corner," Indigo quickly agreed.

"Thank you all. That would be a lovely end to this emotional service."

As Sally turned to follow the others out of the church, she saw Jace Logan and smiled. Since he hadn't stopped to say hello, she knew he was working. Officially, as lead detective on Lisa's murder investigation, Jace was assigned as her protection detail. Until the trial was over, they had to keep their growing personal relationship a secret.

Continuing on her way out of the church, for some reason Sally looked up to the balcony and watched as the broad back of the man she had spotted earlier leave. She didn't know why that was unsettling. First spotting him wearing sunglasses in doors, then seeing Jace, then that queer feeling of being watched. *This memorial service has me spooked.*

Chapter 2

Deep into the early pages of her book, Sally was surprised by the ringing of her doorbell. One of the things she loved about living in a New York City high-rise was that people called ahead or were announced by the doorman. They didn't just drop in unannounced, so she had no idea who it might be. Opening her door, she saw Susan Clark and because she lived in the building didn't have to be announced.

"Susan. This is a pleasant surprise," she said with a welcoming smile for the older woman. It had been a week since they had met for tea following the memorial service for her niece.

"Sally, hi. I know this is sudden, but I wondered if you had a little time. There is something that is niggling at me, and you just might be able to help."

Sally saw the forced smile hid something more serious than a neighborly visit. Since she was the one who spotted something amiss in their building's elevator that turned out to be the body of Susan's niece, they had gotten to know one another, and Sally now counted her as a friend.

After Sally settled the serious-looking woman in the living room, she sat in a nearby chair, glad she had cleared her book and cup of coffee from the side table before answering the door. "Now, how may I be of help?"

"Actually, I was wondering if you might be interested in an idea I had. I was going through Lisa's things, now that the police have released the apartment back to me, and found a couple of notebooks. In each one, the beginning third was simply family recipes. But as I flipped through the pages, I found notes on that book she was working on."

Sally caught her breath. The only information they had was that Lisa was working on an exposé about money laundering and was murdered by Aiden Rafkin and his grandmother, Lorenza. A third family member, Mrs. Rafkin's son Al, was also arrested for the crime of forgery. All three were awaiting trial. "You think Lisa really found enough to prove these people were involved in money laundering? Right now, the family is only accused of her murder."

"Yes. These notes showed that the Rafkin family was involved in something, but there isn't anything specific. Yet Lisa must have uncovered a crime of such magnitude that she frightened someone. Why else would she have been murdered?"

"You've got my attention," Sally replied, wondering what Susan was after. Because she had seen the cloth on the floor of the elevator before the doors had closed in her face and promptly reported it to the doorman, she unknowingly had spotted Lisa's body. The doorman quickly closed down the elevator and called the police. If she'd been even ten minutes later, the killer would have had time to remove the body and no one would have been any the wiser.

"You know, I have always felt somewhat connected to your niece. Even though we'd never met, she became personal to me. So, if you are truly going to finish her research, I would love to help."

"Where do we begin?" Susan said with a warm smile.

"Well, how about a cup of tea?" Sally said with enthusiasm.

With tea and cookies set before them on the kitchen table, Susan pulled out a secretarial notebook and pen, and looked far more relaxed. "I have never written a book. Nor am I familiar with police tactics or procedures. Balancing my bank account is the scope of my mathematical capabilities," she said, pausing as if waiting for Sally to respond. "So, maybe we could complete Lisa's research, and you could write the book? There I've said it!"

"Phew. Write a book? The money aspect of any research would be fun and certainly in my skill set," Sally mused. "But a book? One that would do your niece justice?"

"Couldn't we take it one step at a time? I'm good at organization, research, and compiling reports."

"Well, we'd have to find out what the Rafkins were really up to. Where they hid their ill-gotten gains, large enough to require money being hidden or laundered. In today's world where the government knows everything, how would they have done it?" Sally wondered aloud, noticing that Susan had been taking notes.

"Before I retired, I was an executive assistant to a senior member of a publishing house. I could get a hold of the synopsis of some of our top-selling crime novelists," Susan suggested. "My boss always said that puzzling out a plot for a crime novel was often more thorough than reading about a real crime in the newspapers."

"Didn't you tell me that Lisa had hoped the book would get her a spot with a major newspaper, maybe even *The New York Times*? If that's so, and knowing her research found something truly dangerous, maybe that's why she was so secretive," Sally offered.

"Possibly. She did say telling me more would put me in danger." Taking a bite of a cookie, Susan smiled. "You know, Sally, as a young girl, I would buy her mystery novels for her birthday. She said she loved to figure out who the criminals were before the author revealed them on the page. Once, I gave her a romance novel. Her reaction was so funny. *Really, as if I'd ever read a book like this.* I just laughed, but never bought her anything but crime novels again."

"Well, her murder certainly confirms the theory that this Rafkin family was up to something big. I don't think the police have figured that out. I guess just finding Lisa's murderers was enough to bring the Rafkins to trial."

Sally sat quietly for a couple of minutes, trying to make up her mind. But Susan was trusting her with her niece's legacy;

she had to know. "Susan, on a personal note, remember that nice detective, Jace Logan? Well, I've been seeing him… So, maybe I could talk to him and see what they uncovered when they made their arrests?" Sally said.

"I've seen you two together and hoped it was more personal than solving Lisa's murder. You just look so right together," Susan added.

"About that. To make sure that as a possible witness I'm not compromised, Jace has the department's permission to act as my boyfriend… A cover to protect me. So while it looks personal, no one can know that we are more than friends."

"Not a word. Promise. Nothing must let those criminals go free. I couldn't live with myself." Susan's anguish was clearly heard in her voice.

Chapter 3

Sally had woken earlier than usual. Her mind was a tumble of thoughts. How would one go about hiding large sums of money? Showered, dressed, and coffee brewing, she settled at her desk. *Now where did I put my notes on money laundering?* Following the money was going to hopefully provide clues to the enormity of the crimes Lisa Clark was investigating.

Sally shuffled through her slush file of clipped articles on the subject of money. As a bystander in Lisa's case, she wanted to learn what she could about the topic. While she was an accountant, all her work was done within legal and financial guidelines. It would never occur to her to work with a client who wanted her to alter their books. It was a matter of ethics.

In skimming her file of articles, she remembered one article had an appendix of references. *I guess it was an online search that gave me that list of things to look into. Shit. I didn't save it.*

Just how much money was involved? One million, ten million dollars, Sally wondered. *Let's see, if I had ten bundles of $100 dollar bills, that would measure approximately 13x12x4 inches. A large briefcase would hold that amount of cash, but Jace said the police hadn't found any large sums of* *money on the premises of Rafkin and Sons Antiquarian Books. All their sales records were on computerized files.* If she remembered correctly, not even a scrap of paper or second set of books were found to provide clues as to how much or where funds were being laundered.

Offshore banking took a hit when the US government began to make deals with countries known to assist American citizens in keeping their banking information out of the hands of the IRS. Andorra may be the only country left that was exempt from those agreements. Okay—check the latest banking regulations.

With the inroads in electronic banking, hiding dollars in bearer bonds became unattractive. Didn't I read somewhere that not only were they cumbersome but took too long to transfer for either savings or investment purposes? Anyway, the identity of the person converting bearer bonds to cash would be known.

What would the drug cartels do? They have hundreds of millions to keep from government scrutiny. I saw a movie where they had the cash converted into something called an added-value card. It looked like a plastic debit card but wasn't connected to the user. Hence the owner remained unknown and outside the traditional banking system. I'll have to look into that.

Lately the newspapers are filled with stories about cryptocurrencies. I guess that is my next area of research, Sally thought, packing her laptop in her tote. First stop New York's Midtown Library.

Just as she was pulling on her coat and swinging her tote onto her shoulder, the phone rang. "Sally, this is Susan. I hoped you would be available for a trip to Lisa's apartment. I can show you her notebooks, and maybe we can find something that the police hadn't discovered. It's probably not politically correct, but men and women do think differently," she added with a chuckle.

"Well, I was just about to go to the library to do some research. Would now be a good time?"

"Great. Give me twenty minutes and I'll meet you in the lobby."

As she hung up the phone, Sally wondered what Lisa's home was like. *She worked for a community newspaper and was probably earning less than industry standard. I know how expensive this city is. Was she as clever in furnishing her home as she was in her articles?*

It had been over three years since she moved into the city and, looking around her apartment, realized that it was attractively furnished with a mix of furniture styles, but pristine. *That's a funny thing to think! Why is that idea bothering me?*

With time to spare, Sally took her laptop out of her tote and replaced it with a pad and pen. "Okay, Lisa. I'm on your side. Let Susan and I help you write that book."

Chapter 4

Susan Clark opened the door to a sun-filled studio apartment on the third floor of a walk-up in a section of Manhattan known as Alphabet City. Located on the east side, the streets were numbered, but the avenues were identified by letters, giving the neighborhood its colorful name. In a constantly changing city, this was one of the older areas resisting the encroaching takeover by developers building new high-rise apartment buildings.

"I expected the police to have left the apartment in a mess," Sally said as she walked into the entry. "It looks as if Lisa had just left for work."

"I did find the apartment tossed around, and quickly restored it… you know, out of respect for my niece. She once told me that she was lucky her mom raised her to be neat as there was no extra space for even a sweater tossed on a chair. Look, I'm going to start going through her dresser. Let me know if you find anything."

Sally approved of the neatly decorated apartment where every inch of space was utilized. And yet, Lisa had managed to make the twelve-by-twenty-foot space comfortable. A small efficiency kitchen was built into one wall of the entryway, and next to it, a small door leading into a bathroom the size of a small closet. The main room was separated into work and living spaces by the placement of inexpensive catalogue furniture. The work area contained all the outlets needed for electronic devices. And, off to one side, was an alcove with a neatly made-up daybed and small bedside tables on either side.

Sally tried to envision living in such a compact space. She would have all the basics for living, but storage would be a huge problem. She wouldn't have room for all her pots and pans, let alone her collection of spices. But, still, the place didn't feel claustrophobic. *Maybe I'd paint the one wall without cabinets in a cheerful yellow, instead of institutional white. But that's all.*

"Susan, I think Jace told me that Lisa had a flash drive hidden in the drapery rod. After that they checked both windows, even the curtain rod in the bathroom, but didn't find anything."

Stopping her search of a cabinet with t-shirts and sweaters, Susan turned and looked at Sally. "You know, we women pack things away and each of us has our own system. So why don't we just look around. Who knows what we'll find. I put the notebooks I told you about over on the coffee table."

Sally took a moment to gather her bearings. "Okay. I'll start in the kitchen." As she opened the upper cabinet with only two shelves, she pulled out each of the containers to see if they could have had false bottoms. She had read about older people hiding their jewelry to prevent home care workers from finding their valuables. But there weren't any. After running her hand over the shelf under the containers of coffee and other dry foods, she moved on to the bottom of the cabinet that contained a stack of dishes in three sizes. Removing all twelve dishes from dinner plates to cereal bowls, she placed them on the stovetop and restacked them one by one. As she laid out the last plate, she saw a slip of paper and a key. *Oh my, a receipt and key for a safe deposit box.*

"Susan, look at this!" she all but shouted. "Have we hit the jackpot? Do you have power of attorney so we might gain access to Lisa's safe deposit box?" Her excitement conveyed hope as she handed both items to Susan.

"I think so. Let me call Steven Pressman, my attorney, for advice," Susan said, and dialing, her cell was quickly connected. "Steven, this is Susan Clark. I'm over at my niece's apartment and found a key to a safe deposit box. Will my power of attorney gain me access?"

The voice was loud enough for Sally to hear the attorney's end of the conversation. "Actually, Susan, no. Not until you finalize the estate papers, one of which names you executor. And that gives you authority to act on behalf of your niece's estate."

Sally saw Susan's confused expression and hesitation before she replied, "I don't understand."

"When your niece passed away, her assets automatically passed into her estate. All activities on behalf of the estate can be authorized by the executor, which, in this case, is you. So stop by my office tomorrow afternoon and I will have the papers ready to sign. After they're filed, you will be able to access Lisa's bank accounts, the apartment, and everything else in her estate."

"That's clear enough. I wonder why we haven't done this before?" Susan, now clearly upset, was gripping her cell phone more tightly.

"I guess because you only notified me of her death last week. But not to worry. I'll take care of it." Susan clicked off her cell and stood silently; her hand shook slightly as she pocketed the phone. "I was so focused on finding out who killed Lisa, I guess it never occurred to me to get in touch with my lawyer."

"Let's focus on looking for clues. Maybe we will find something else. I must say I'm encouraged," Sally said.

Susan looked up and realized she hadn't looked in the closet outside the bathroom. It couldn't have been more than four feet wide, and maybe one and a half feet in depth, but Lisa had neatly fit her clothes into the small space. After going through all pockets and lifting clothes off the upper shelf, she put everything back as it was and closed the door.

Meanwhile, Sally was focused on the built-in cabinets covering the long wall opposite the daybed. Fitted neatly into the design was a nook and built-in desk. Beginning at the window, she carefully opened each cabinet and searched not only its contents but ran her hand over the doors and interior walls. On the last cabinet next to the desk, Sally's finger touched a piece of tape. It must be the back of the screw, she thought. Opening the door wider, she saw a slight shape under

What She Didn't Know 3

tape that blended in with the rest of the cabinet and gently peeled it away. "Holy shit," she exclaimed. In her hand was a memory card small enough to hide from someone who didn't know what to look for. "Susan. Look at this!"

Susan rushed to Sally's side and the first time since speaking to her lawyer, broke out in a huge grin. Looking up at Sally, she laughed. "Now we have the notebooks, this memory card, and by next week a safety deposit box to investigate."

An hour later, they hadn't found anything more. "I can at least begin to get us organized. Why don't I take the safe deposit key and notebooks. I'll assemble those notes and make copies for you," Susan said.

"Okay. I'll take the memory card, make copies for each of us, and we can meet to see what we have. Maybe there's enough information to learn the magnitude of the criminal activities that so fascinated Lisa."

Sally was lost in thought. "You know, Susan, here I am going through all of Lisa's personal things and I don't even know what she was like."

Smiling, Susan walked over to the bookshelf and reaching up, pulled down a small photo album. "Let me introduce you two." Opening the book, she turned a few pages until she came upon a photo of a younger version of herself standing next to a handsome man. "This is my wedding photo showing Lisa's Uncle Walter," she said, touching the photo reverently. Turning a few more pages, she said, "And here are Lisa and me at her college graduation. We were the only family left. Her parents had perished in a car crash two years earlier, and I lost the love of my life shortly thereafter."

Then Susan brightened. "And this is my favorite picture of Lisa." It was a studio photo of a smiling, sweet-faced young woman.

"She doesn't look anything like a hard-nosed reporter," Sally remarked.

"Lisa once told me that smiling and being friendly was one of her gifts. She said that given the opportunity, most people loved talking about themselves. That and her ability to read people were the skills that set her apart as a journalist."

"Maybe we are on the road to restoring Lisa's dream of publishing her exposé, and getting the attention of *The New York Times*."

"Oh how she would have loved it if that were true," Susan replied wistfully. "How about lunch on me? I think we need a break. I know I do."

Chapter 5

High on the success of her day with Susan Clark, Sally headed over to Jeanne and Ryan's for dinner. During the past few months, they had become as close-knit as if they had grown up together. She was happy about Jeanne finally finding that special man; and who would have ever imagined it to be her brother-in-law, Ryan Scott? So where he had been a good and trusted friend, they were now a close family.

Sally was greeted with a hug from Jeanne and thought she smelled something cooking in the kitchen. "A sidecar, girlfriend?" Sally said in surprise, accepting the cocktail. Jeanne knew she usually drank wine. Taking a sip, she smiled. "Well done. Just what I needed."

"It looks like we've turned you away from wine and onto mixed drinks. And you know, I don't care as long as you're happy," Jeanne added.

Sally, filled with love, hugged her best friend, giving her a swift kiss on the cheek. "You can do anything you want. I'm all yours."

Ryan joined his wife, giving Sally a hug of his own. "This is the huggingest family ever," he said with a wide grin. Taking

Sally's coat, he led her into the living room where Jace stood, and who added his own warm hug.

Amazed wasn't the right word. While she knew Jace and Ryan had become friends, this was different; it was a family dinner. Just because she and Jace were seeing each other, she wasn't ready for the rest to know about it.

"We asked Jace to join us," Jeanne said, with a twinkle in her eye.

Sally was fully aware she was being watched for a reaction. "Ryan, Jeanne, this *is* a nice surprise." *She's just matchmaking. Now that she's happily married, she wants the same for me.*

Before things got too adult, Jane and Mark rushed over with more hugs for Sally, leaving her a bit breathless. "I swear, even though I saw you both two weeks ago, you've grown." Their huge grins told Sally she couldn't have said anything they would have liked more.

Turning to Ryan, she asked, "Why is it these two can't wait to grow up? Do they have any clue how wonderful they have it now?" That sparked laughter on the part of all the adults with the kids just looking puzzled.

"Jeanne, what's up at the office?" Sally asked as she settled on the sofa next to Jace, who quietly reached for her hand.

"I had the nicest of days. That COVID patient who had been with us for six months came to see me for his final paperwork. You know the balance of his bill after insurance paid their share and post-hospital treatment instructions included scheduling of some physical therapy. I was happy to tell him that the balance after insurance wasn't that bad and the hospital had agreed to let him pay it back in monthly installments. His grin just warmed me from the inside out."

Sally looked to Ryan, who was clearly pleased with the way things turned out. "My wife is an example of just how much can be accomplished if you truly care for the people you work with."

Feeling Jace's arm around her shoulder, all Sally could do was look up and smile. "And you, good sir. Have you slain any dragons today?"

At that Mark shouted, "Oh, Detective Logan, tell us the criminals you arrested," the boy so eager to hear all the details. "Well, young man, first call me Jace. And, no dragons, but I did help a woman at a supermarket retrieve her handbag from a bad guy with a gun."

"Wow. I want to do that when I grow up," Mark said, clearly impressed with his new role model.

"You know what will make you a great detective?" Jace asked, seeing that Mark had moved to his side. "Being the best student in school. That will be good practice when you begin to study all those procedures you will need to do the best job you can. Once you catch your criminal, you have to do everything by the book to make sure that person stays caught."

Sally looked over to Ryan, clearly pleased with the way the conversation had turned.

"So, Sally, you said you had a good day," Ryan began. "What was so special? A new client?"

"I do have a lead on a possible new client. But no. Mrs. Clark asked me to help finish her niece's research and write that book she was working on." She hadn't expected the complete silence that greeted her news.

"Sally, do you know what you're undertaking?" Jace asked.

"Not really. I thought you might help me sort it out." Her request was met with a thoughtful nod.

"Unfortunately, my help is limited. As long as you are a potential witness, I'm unable to talk to you about the case. If it's known that I've discussed any aspects of the investigation with you, their attorney could get the case thrown out and the criminals would go free."

"It's just research. You know the internet and public library," Sally countered, clearly not expecting Jace's resistance.

"You had better protect her from her own curiosity. I haven't been able to stop her from pursuing anything she sets her mind to," Ryan said in a firm voice. Jace knew it was an order. The two men had become fast friends, the kind who understood the meaning behind even the mildest of comments.

"Dinner is ready," Jeanne announced. "Jane made place cards. We are being a bit more formal tonight," she said with a laugh.

"I tried to think of a design you would all like, and with Christmas around the corner, I chose a pine cone," Jane announced.

"Christmas. This year, everyone, it will be at the Ryan Scotts. I will send out invitations, including one to Barbara. And, Sally, you can bring one of your fabulous pies, Jace wine, and we will take care of the rest." Jeanne's invitation was greeted with a loud round of applause.

They all gathered around the table set with the china Sally had given the happy couple as a wedding present. The crisp white tablecloth and gleaming silver flatware made a festive setting for Jeanne's dinner. "I haven't seen a table so beautifully set in years," gushed Sally.

As dishes were passed around, the conversation reverted to Christmas, with everyone adding their special contributions toward making it a truly festive celebration. Jane and Mark insisted on going shopping to get new lights and extra ornaments. Jeanne and Sally shared menu ideas. "Jace, I think we've been forgotten," Ryan said. With a mischievous smile, added, "We might go shopping. You know, a guy thing."

Jace's reaction wasn't in keeping with the mood of happy party planners. "Thank you, Ryan, but I am afraid I won't be able to join you. I always take the Christmas shift so my fellow officers can be with their families." Then brightening, added, "But shopping. I'm sure we can schedule something."

"It's settled. No women," Ryan proclaimed with a hearty laugh.

"Then you will all join me for New Year's Eve," Sally happily proclaimed, and seeing Jace nod in agreement, knew he would do everything he could to make it.

Chapter 6

Sally pulled her rental car into an almost empty cemetery parking lot, turned off the engine, and sat lost in thought. When she owned a car, her trips to visit Tyler's grave had been more frequent. But today, while sad, there was a purpose behind this visit.

Then, turning to Jeanne, she smiled. "Thank you for accompanying me. This is a difficult visit. The entire drive out here, I was trying to figure out how to tell Tyler I had to move on with my life. It's been a confusing several months."

"You know, Sally, visiting Tyler's grave has a different feeling now that I'm family. When I married Ryan, I also became an aunt to Tyler's son and daughter. Not to mention your sister-in-law... not just your best friend."

Sally reached over and gave Jeanne's shoulder a pat. Then, saying a silent prayer, unbuckled her seat belt.

"How often do you visit Tyler?" Jeanne asked.

"That first year I came out here every week. Then after the move to the apartment, once a month. But Lisa Clark's murder changed all that. My life was no longer in my control. I didn't stop thinking of Tyler, not for a minute. In a way he's still with me, even if I couldn't visit his grave."

"Did Ryan tell you that we visited the cemetery on the first anniversary of Tyler's death? That was three years ago, and Ryan wanted Jane and Mark to remember their uncle. He wanted to pick up Judy and Billy from their home in New Jersey and bring them as well. But…"

"But Victoria wouldn't let you," Sally said, finishing Jeanne's thought. It was a statement of fact. "I miss those two. They deserve so much more. Oh, Jeanne, I so wanted to adopt them. But… Vicious Vickie won't let them near me." Sally's words were sharp with loss.

"On another note, Ryan was going to ask you to join us. But he told me you seemed isolated in your grief and didn't want to intrude on your privacy."

"Is that what I was? Isolated?" Sally didn't think of her life that way. She was simply keeping to herself and building a business. It took all of her attention.

"Have you gotten over all Tyler's secrets? That affair, his burgeoning debt?" Jeanne asked.

Sally's head swung around with eyes focused on her friend and on seeing nothing but gentleness, relaxed. "Jeanne, I was partially to blame. If I hadn't been pushing to get pregnant, maybe I'd have seen that Tyler didn't think he could support any more children, no matter how much he would have loved them. If I'd known that, I could have gone back to work and he wouldn't have had to work so hard," she said closing her eyes and picturing the calendar she'd found after Tyler's death marking her fertile days… those days he made sure he wasn't home to turn their lovemaking into a pregnancy.

Gathering her thoughts, Sally opened the car door and looked over to her best friend. "Let's make this a happy visit. OK?" Her lighter tone cleared the sorrowful mood.

The two women walked from the parking lot along the pebble-strewn pathway. It was mid-morning and the sun was warming the chilled air. Approaching a small horizontal granite gravestone, they saw the simple wording: Tyler William Scott, 1980–2020. Beloved Husband and Father.

"You chose a simple marker so very like Tyler," Jeanne remarked.

"Uh huh," Sally said, thinking of the slim man in his tailored suits, not a spare bit of embellishment, just like the plain gravestone she'd selected. Placing a small stone on top of the headstone, she said a silent prayer of farewell.

Sweetheart, you were and are the first love of my life. I treasure your passion, the care you took to make our life together one of warmth, and for sharing Judy and Billy with me. It's been a sad five years without you and during that time, real life insisted on crashing into my serenity. I've told you all about the murder investigation and the kindness of Detective Jace Logan. What I haven't been able to tell you is that we've fallen in love. It's a different kind of love, no less deep, but because you are both different men, my love is shaded with different colors and activities. I hope I have your blessings.

Sally stepped up and placed her hand gently over Tyler's name, then threw him a kiss. Straightening up, she felt relieved. *It's not goodbye, Love.* Feeling lighter, she put her arm around Jeanne's shoulder and gave her a warm smile. "Thank you for helping me say goodbye."

Chapter 7

Returning to her apartment, Sally's mind focused on Tyler, and conflicting emotions about her new desire to fully love Jace. Looking over to a small table, she spotted a silver-framed photo of Tyler. "Handsome. My prince. My love." Then glancing at other frames, walked to the table, and picked up Jeanne and Ryan's wedding photo, caressing the picture of her two favorite people in her small world. There were two smaller frames and lifting one from the table, she smiled at the faces of all four children, then spotted her mom, Barbara, in their midst. *The kids all call you Gram.*

Still lost in thought, she suddenly realized that the family she so wanted, she had. She could count on Ryan's always being there to help her out, but never smothering her with advice. And while she and Jeanne had been roommates all those years ago, they were each living different lives. Sally working for Tyler and their budding romance, and Jeanne wrapped up in her career at the hospital. *Now you are family. My family. Even our conversations are different.*

As Sally looked up at her pristinely kept home, it looked empty. Yes, it was nicely furnished. Yes, it was spacious for an apartment in Manhattan. But it didn't echo with laughter, where children were clamoring for attention and adults trying to keep the din at reasonable levels. *Family. Yes, I get it.*

"Scrapbooks," Sally exclaimed as she went to the bookcase in her office and pulled out the four photo albums she had made for the children. They contained photos that Tyler took on that disastrous trip to Antarctica. The photo she chose for the cover was of a smiling Tyler holding his camera. She was going to give the albums to the children over Thanksgiving, but somehow forgot. Jeanne's Christmas party would be the perfect time to talk about Tyler and their trip to the White World. Five years had passed since he had slipped and died at the bottom of a crevasse in the snow-covered landscape trying to get just that right angle for another photo. This would be a celebratory gift, something to spark shared memories of earlier times.

As she laid out the books, Sally wanted to add to the note she had already written for each child and placed at the beginning of each book. One for each... Judy, Billy, Jane, and Mark.

"Now where are those magnets we brought in Ushuaia? Ah, in my travel kit." Pulling the small zippered case she fit into the side pocket of her carry-on suitcase, Sally smiled as the half dozen little figurines fell onto her bed.

"OK, the rubber zodiac for Billy, our ship for Mark, penguin for Judy, and seal for Jane." The magnets had small holes that enabled her to thread them through the ribbons she used to finish off each elaborately wrapped package.

Fully pleased with her day that started at the cemetery and ended with a gift that celebrated her love for Tyler and their family. "Hot bath, then a glass of wine, and I think I'm going to order a pizza. Indulgent. So what," she decided, wearing a smile of satisfaction.

* * *

While lying in the bath covered in bubbles, Sally's thoughts turned to Jace. He wasn't happy about her book project. *What will he do when he learns what we found in Lisa's apartment?*

Closing her eyes didn't help her conflict. Today's visit to the cemetery resolved one problem; yes, she loved Jace. Now she needed to do something to cement their relationship. But she was already violating Jace's warning that he had to distance himself or she'd be a compromised witness at the Rafkins' trial. Shit. Whenever that would be?

I'm damned if I do and damned if I don't. And that thought won't get me anywhere. How would I solve this if it was a business problem? Paper and pen. Two columns, one you do and one you don't.

OK. The <u>You Do</u> column wins. Throw caution to the wind and commit to loving Jace.

The <u>You Don't</u> column. You don't hide anything you find in your research from Jace. Especially the memory card and key to that safe deposit box.

35

Chapter 8

Sally had tossed and turned all night. By five, when sleep was no longer possible, she headed for the kitchen and coffee. *I'd infuse it if I could.* Two hours and two strong cups of coffee later, she called Jace.

"Good morning, Jace. I wonder if you would like to come up for dinner tonight? I'll make salmon. You probably want to know more about that book Susan Clark wants me to work on."

"Yes. And I'll bring wine along with my curiosity."

Hanging up the phone, Sally's hand remained on the receiver, not wanting to break her connection with Jace. Thankfully, he had been so matter-of-fact in accepting her invitation, she hoped he would be understanding when he heard what they had found.

She was dressed in slacks and a sweater. A tailored look she hoped would show the seriousness of the evening's conversation. But when she opened the door at the ring of her bell and Jace swept her up in a full-body hug, all thoughts vanished. All she could do was feel sensations that had her tingling down to her toes. "Whew. I'm not sure I'm going to be capable of preparing that dinner," she whispered nervously.

Keeping both of his arms around her shoulders, Jace's face had a glow. "I'm hungry for something different from salmon."

"Yes," was her breathy reply. And leading him into the bedroom, Sally slowly pulled him close, teased his lips with her tongue, and sighed.

Had Jace hesitated? But as his hands slowly traveled over her breasts, and her nipples hardened, she knew that finally, she was going to have the man who had confused and fascinated her for months. She was in no hurry.

As Jace's hands switched to her back and moved gently under her sweater, she felt her bra give way.

"I have to feel you next to me," she said in tones so low they were more of a wish.

"Yes." It didn't take Jace long to remove her sweater and pull off his own. His hands, warm on her skin, began to circle first her breasts, then moving to her waist, unbuttoned her slacks. Standing before him, slacks pooled at her ankles, she stood expectantly in her underpants. The tingling of her heated flesh demanding more. Before she could move, he'd stripped off his pants and lifting her in his arms, kicked their clothes aside, and placed her on the bed.

"I want to look at all of you. I've dreamed about holding you, kissing your entire body for months. I don't want to rush it now."

His voice was seductive. Sally was lost. Feelings built to a crescendo with their slow coupling that heated to their climactic release, and then the sweetest of merging in a full-body embrace, where both fell asleep.

* * *

At two a.m., Sally had finished preparing their belated dinner, sipping wine while stealing kisses from Jace.

With the table set and dinner served, Sally looked up and noticed the mood had changed from sexy to Jace's normally easy-going but quiet one. She knew that when he had something important to say, he would speak up.

"I hope your silence isn't because you're worried about my cooking?" she teased. Trying to lighten his mood and stop him from thinking of the reason she had invited him to dinner. The book.

"Ah, no. Just thinking about your new project. If you know what you will be getting into."

"Of course. And I love you for worrying about me." He would certainly be worried, but that could wait. Right now, she wanted to stay in the afterglow of their new intimacy. Smiling, she leaned down and gave Jace a deep kiss, then refilled his glass of wine.

"Delicious. You, my dear, could open a restaurant," Jace said as he happily devoured his meal.

The look she adored had returned with his compliment. "My pleasure is in cooking for an appreciative audience of one, or lately, my family of seven."

With another sip of her wine, she began fiddling with her fork, but stopped because Jace had already told her it was a habit she had when she was worried about something. Looking over, she saw him waiting for her to get to the point.

"So, Susan Clark stopped by and said that while you caught Lisa's murderer, she wanted to finish the book that had cost her niece's life. It had been her driving passion and well-kept secret." *Damn it, he's just sitting there, waiting.*

"Now, don't be defensive, but she also said that men and women looked at their homes differently. That while you found the flash drive, Lisa may have had more information hidden somewhere in her apartment."

At that, Jace raised an eyebrow, but still didn't comment.

"Well, she went on to tell me that when she was straightening up Lisa's apartment after the police released it to her, she found several notebooks. On thumbing through each, she noticed that the first third of the pages contained recipes, but on a few inner pages were carefully written notes about Lisa's research into money laundering and Rafkin and Sons Antiquarian Books."

Another raised eyebrow. I'd better hurry and get to the rest.

39

"She then asked me to visit the apartment with her... and we did." Looking down at the fork she was moving around her plate, she cleared her throat. "And, well, we did find a couple of other little items." Sally was rushing to hide a half-truth... that the items weren't little at all but could be a major breakthrough in the mystery of Lisa and her book.

"Now we get to it," Jace said in a tightly controlled voice.

"A memory card and a key to a safe deposit box." *There it's all out in the open. Why is he just sitting there?*

"Before you ask what was on the memory card, or in the safe deposit box, I don't know. I haven't looked at the card. Until Susan is officially named executor of Lisa's estate, she can't go to the bank and gain access to that box and its secrets. In the meantime, Susan is in the process of writing up a summary of the information she found in those notebooks."

"Is that all?"

"Ah... well, I didn't want to look at the memory card without you."

"And you want to know if you should turn over that information to me." It was a statement, not a question.

"Um."

"Would it make things easier if you just showed me the notebooks and memory card? And then I talked to you both before you continued any further?"

"Maybe, but you know my curiosity... so why don't we go to the computer and both see what those zeros and ones are hiding? Does it contain names and places of whatever the Rafkins were involved with? You said that the investigation still hadn't found anything connected to money laundering."

Jace just smiled. "Why wait any longer? I might get distracted," he teased.

"Oh, if I wasn't mad for your kisses, I'd love you for understanding," she said, relief in every word.

Sally had wanted Jace to share her discovery all along. He was the expert in uncovering secrets. This time she would be part of solving the puzzle, not merely a bystander who found a dead woman in her building's elevator.

Hugging her robe so it fit more tightly to her body, Sally rushed to her office and, with a quick glance at Jace, smiled. He looked like he did in her dreams… his body hard and ripped above the waist of his slacks. "And this is my office," she said, as if Jace needed any explanation. But it redirected her mind off his body and to the task ahead.

As she turned on her computer and inserted the little card, Jace moved behind her chair, bending down to get a better angle on the monitor. The opening document was labeled *businesses*. And with a click, they viewed a diagram listing of names. Top of the pyramid was Allied Investments. Sub listings were also names of businesses: Allied Realty, Allied Construction, and Allied Shipping.

The next file titled *to be researched,* included the following questions: Look into each of the businesses for websites, company officers, locations, official documentation.

"Jace, that's all there is." Sally's disappointment was clearly visible in her frown.

"Yes, but while I know you are going to look into each of those areas, I have contacts that can help with a wider search. Tax filings, certificates of business, and criminal activities associated with any of these companies."

"You don't mind Susan and I looking into this information?" Sally asked in surprise. She had been left out of the information loop during Jace's murder investigation. He only told a little bit at any one time, but never enough to satisfy her need to know why the young reporter had been killed. His explanation was that if he divulged information about the case against the Rafkins, it might taint the evidence he gathered and the murderer could go free.

"As if I could keep you from sticking your nose into these notes on your own," Jace teased, and leaned down with the softest of kisses. "Now make a copy for yourself, and give me the original." As Jace left the computer with a light-hearted smile, Sally needed more. "Ah… Jace?" she said, slowing his steps away from her desk. "Would you share some of that information with us? Nothing that would jeopardize the case… but I will want to follow these leads to see where they go."

"For you, my love. I will try to help your research," Jace whispered and kissed her lightly on the cheek. She just sat there. Not wanting their time together to end.

After copying the memory card and handing him the original, Sally's gaze returned to Jace's torso, her hands just wanting to touch every indentation. "You know, I have dessert if you don't have to leave right away."

"I was thinking that it's Sunday and I should be spending my time in leisurely pursuits, not working."

"Oh?" She didn't have time to say another word as Jace's lips fastened on hers. "Sweet," he murmured, lifting Sally from the chair and pulling her into his arms.

Chapter 9

"OK, girlfriend. Spill it. What did you think of Ryan's idea of inviting Jace to dinner the other night?" Jeanne teased over the phone. Sally was accustomed to Jeanne's prodding for intimate details, smiling on hearing her follow-up, "You didn't look displeased."

Jeanne's voice filled with mischief warmed Sally's heart. Jace had left around ten that morning, and she had hit the bed for another couple hours of sleep. Just the mention of his name made her body tingle. *It's too soon to share my happiness.*

"Actually, I was glad you all got along. It was fun." Sally would share more with Jeanne, but only in person and not right away. She wanted to treasure her newfound discovery. Loving Jace filled her with a happiness she hadn't known since Tyler's death. Five long years of hiding from life.

Sally refocused on what Jeanne was saying. "You know Ryan is mad about him. Told me that Jace was not only honest, but he could see when they first met that he had a gleam in his eyes when they talked about you."

"How could Ryan know Jace might have been interested in me?" Sally asked with faked surprise. "I've only just been able to unscramble my brain and realize he's charming." *Charming and so much more.*

"Well, you did put up all those defenses. No matter how I tried to get you out of your isolated widowhood, you stayed within the safety of your apartment."

"Jeanne, you know me so well. And I did listen. I went to a museum and took a trip all by myself," Sally replied defensively.

"It took a murder to break you out of your shell and I don't care; it brought you back to life. So come over tonight for Sunday dinner. I'm ordering pizza. We can all play a game. I'll let Jane and Mark choose one of their favorites."

"That's just the perfect ending to my weekend," Sally replied, chuckling. *If you only knew.*

* * *

"You guys, this was a wonderful evening. Pizza, games, and family," Sally said, sipping an after-dinner coffee. Kids in bed and just Jeanne and Ryan to herself.

"We were thinking of Christmas," Jeanne began. "The plans we discussed the other day need time. Shopping, invitations… you know Jane is set on designing them. And then seeing what your mom wants to do. She loves the kids so much, I'm afraid of all the gifts she'll get. If the kids didn't love her before, Christmas surely will clinch the deal."

"I know she would love to do a real Christmas, like we had before my dad passed away," Sally said, picturing her mom in full festive mode. "Let me call her. I know she'll love it and she can stay with me. If I know Mom, after she sees your tree, she's going to scold me for not having one myself." Then laughed at the thought.

"Jeanne. Can Ryan get Victoria to let the kids stay over for the Christmas vacation from school? I know it would mean so much to them," Sally asked. If she was forbidden to have her stepdaughter and stepson visit, maybe Ryan could work a miracle and have Judy and Billy visit them.

"What are you two planning now?" Ryan asked as he brought his coffee over and sat down.

"Darling, do you think you could get Victoria to let the kids stay with us for the Christmas week?" Jeanne asked.

"Oh, Ryan, it would make everything almost perfect," Sally chimed in. "That vixen won't let me near my own stepchildren. I love them. She certainly doesn't," Sally burst out in frustration.

"Don't fret. Victoria seems less and less interested in controlling their lives. I'll get her to agree to my picking them up on Saturday for the Christmas holiday. She'll probably be relieved not to have to pretend to be a loving mother and getting a tree that would drop needles on her pristine carpet, not to mention presents when she would rather spend the money on herself."

"Oh, Ryan, thank you," Sally said with a tear or two in her voice.

"We love them too, Sally. It seems that as the senior member of the Scott Family, it's my job to sort out what's important," Ryan added.

"We'll start this Saturday. With Judy and Billy staying over, I'll work with the kids to help plan homemade ornaments; maybe I'll even bring out my knitting needles and make stockings to hang on the fireplace mantel," Jeanne said, reaching for a pad and pen.

"I can finally give the kids their photo albums." Sally loved her step kids and missed spending time with them. They needed her, and she needed them. Maybe now more than ever. They were her connection to Tyler and the family she once had.

The following chatter with everyone talking at once reminded Sally how lucky she was. Jeanne and Ryan and the four children filled her with love and laughter.

"It's too bad Jace can't join us for Christmas," Jeanne said, looking over to see Sally's reaction.

"Yes. Too bad." *Maybe soon.*

"Sally, come on. Give. What's happening with you two?"

She never could hide anything from Jeanne. Sally's smile just lit the room. It was as if the sun had come out after dark. "He slowly and patiently stole my heart."

"Sally, I couldn't be happier," Ryan said and, looking over to his wife, winked.

Chapter 10

Sally had a few hours before she had to meet Indigo to finalize the year-end's numbers. And yet, here she was sitting before her computer, inserting the copy of the memory card from Lisa Clark's apartment. She couldn't help it.

Now let's see what Allied Investments is all about. You seem to be top of the pyramid. Are you a scheme? After a half hour of searching all the databases she was aware of, she hadn't found anything on the company. *I wonder if Susan has made any progress on transcribing Lisa's notes.*

Picking up her cell, she hit Susan's number. "Good morning, Susan. I thought maybe you could meet me around eleven at the Southern Comfort bakery. I have to meet Indigo on some business, but by eleven, we could enjoy her tea room offerings. They are, I promise, fabulous."

"I remember that pretty gal from the memorial service. And tea afterward. Her muffins were heavenly. And, yes, that would be perfect. I finished organizing Lisa's notes and I'll bring you a copy."

"Great. I'll bring the little I found on that memory card and we can compare notes. It wasn't much."

* * *

Laughter over muffins and tea, and Sally's mind wandered. Was that reclusive widow gone forever? Sometimes she hardly recognized herself. Settling back to the conversation at the table, Sally saw Susan pick up her notes on the memory card's contents.

"So, is this a listing of businesses somehow connected to the Rafkins? And are they leads Lisa was beginning to follow?" Susan asked.

"It looks like there are two avenues of research. One: the questions you found listed in Lisa's notebooks. As for the memory card, these must be businesses. But where are they located? Are they legitimate? How do they fit in with Lisa's money laundering thesis? I'm afraid my initial online search this morning was unsuccessful," Sally reported.

"Since you have a relationship with Detective Logan, do you think he could look into these for us?" Susan asked.

"I gave him the original memory card and he said he would look into those companies," Sally replied.

"But will he share what he finds?" Susan's tone expressed doubt.

Sally, however, was hopeful that maybe in this one area, they could work together. "He hadn't said anything about Lisa's secret book impacting his case. And he knows we are only interested in following the money. Yes, maybe, Susan. I'll ask if he's turned up any leads."

"By the way, why haven't those two gone to trial? It's been five months since the Rafkins were arrested," Susan snapped, clearly upset to think that her niece wouldn't be given the justice she deserved. "That man must be convicted and I won't rest until we see him jailed for life."

"Apparently our courts are overloaded. Jace tells me that five months isn't that unusual. In fact, it could take a couple of years to come to trial. Maybe the prosecution is waiting for more information? Or the Rafkins' lawyer is demanding more access? I can at least ask Jace about the delay. Until then, maybe Ryan has a contact," Sally said, making a note on a napkin to call Ryan when she got home.

"Sally, you just gave me a fabulous idea. The publisher I worked for has a top-selling crime novelist, who happens to also be an attorney, and a friend of mine. Let me see if I can set up a meeting for us. Since he has to make these situations up, he might help us to begin our research, or maybe he even has resources we can use."

"Anyone I might know?"

The smile on Susan's face hinted at someone well-known. "Tony Granger."

"You mean the author on everybody's bestseller list? I've read two of his mysteries and couldn't put them down. Even if it wasn't important to our project, just meeting him would be a thrill," Sally gushed.

Susan picked up her cell and called Granger, nodding at the end of the call. "Let's go. Tony is at the office and waiting for us."

* * *

Standing on Third Avenue and looking up at the famous lipstick building—one of New York's more famous office structures—Sally wondered what she and Susan would learn. While she read mostly fiction, it had never occurred to her to wonder how a novelist developed a plot with all the dead ends and mysterious clues designed to keep the reader captivated up until the very end when the criminal and motivation were revealed.

The lobby interior matched the red stone on the building's exterior and off to one side was a coffee bar and placed in front, several small tables. It was approaching the noon hour and people were rushing out of the elevators, one woman nearly knocking Sally aside. "Doesn't anyone in the city ever walk?" Sally asked Susan, who laughed as she stepped into the just-emptied carriage.

"Hi, Tony," Susan said, taking the middle-aged man's hand in a warm handshake. "Let me introduce you to Sally Scott, the friend who is helping me finish my niece's book."

Handsome didn't begin to describe the trim, dark-haired man that up close looked like a banker with a smile that could charm anyone, Sally thought as they shook hands. She was surprised by the man's clean-shaven and polished appearance. His form-fitting three-piece suit with tinted blue shirt and a surprisingly colorful tie had to have been made to order. *Even Tyler's suits weren't this elegant.* Didn't authors work at home in jeans and t-shirts? This man's attire was straight out of *Gentlemen's Quarterly* magazine.

"Ladies, I've ordered tea in the library. Follow me, please," Tony said.

Once settled, Sally took out a notebook and waited. She wasn't quite sure how to begin. This was something entirely outside her skillset. And Mr. Granger was Susan's friend. That was easy to see… they looked so very comfortable together with Susan leaning in to hear every word he said.

"Tony, as I told you on the phone, my niece Lisa Clark was a reporter working on a story about money laundering… for which she was murdered. While the police have her murderer awaiting trial, I was hoping to write that book in her memory."

"Susan, writing a book may look easy, but if you are thinking of solving a crime, that is an entirely different matter," Tony said in softened tones meant to downplay his concern.

Clearing her throat, Sally interrupted. "Mr. Granger, let us fill you in on what we actually know about Lisa's murder and the people involved." Looking over to Susan, she saw that she had her permission to divulge anything she felt important, and proceeded to fill Tony in. "We aren't trying to solve Lisa's murder; the people responsible are awaiting trial. We want to find the key to Lisa's fascination with this family. And all she has told Susan was that it involved money laundering."

Tapping the table with his hand, it took a moment before he replied. "OK. So, these Rafkins, harken back to the infamous New York Italian Mob of the twenties. I've written a couple of novels mentioning their liquor smuggling, murder, extortion, rackets, even prostitution. However, money laundering is a different kettle of fish."

"But…" Sally started to say, stopping when she saw that he wasn't finished.

"Ladies, it isn't hiding the money that is your first problem. You need to know how these people kept large amounts of cash. When you know the scope of those funds, then you have to find their location and see if the money is still being accessed. You may be looking back 100 years and researching all the changes in banking regulations since that time. Look at the drug cartels today. They also run a cash business. So, I'd start by identifying the people at the center of Lisa's research."

"We found some notes and the Italian Mob was on the list of things to look into. We also found names of what may be companies," Sally said.

"Then what I always do is start with the end… in this case, being able to use the hidden money. Then I list the possible people involved… their names, occupations, colleagues… that kind of thing. Sometimes that will indicate a process on which to build the plot. And then outline the plot as if I was the one who arranged to first obtain the illegal funds, and find a way to launder them."

"We believe Mrs. Rafkin, the grandmother of the murderer, is the head of this family. She inherited her role from her father, an associate of Joseph Gambino. We also know that she opened an Antiquarian Book Shop in the early forties."

"You said she inherited her father's business?"

Both women just nodded, waiting for Tony to continue.

"I doubt she'd run a prostitution ring. And smuggling liquor is no longer necessary. So, what besides books could earn large amounts... say in the millions?" Tony asked, more to himself.

"Her son was also arrested for forgery of documents." Sally's soft voice seemingly penetrated the author's silence.

"Forgery? Documents, not money?" Tony asked, surprise showing on his raised eyebrows. "Sally?"

"Yes, please call me Sally."

"You have me intrigued. And I owe Susan for all she has kindly done for me. Typing edited manuscripts to name only one of her gifts to this author who works on an old Underwood typewriter. Let me look into the money aspect. Susan, start researching the New York Mafia of the 1920s. Especially Mrs. Rafkin's family history. What her father did... who he worked for... that sort of thing. And, Sally, why not try to trace those businesses?"

Sally and Susan simply nodded. It was a start. But she could hear Ryan in her head, warning her not to get involved... that Lisa Clark had been murdered over this very story. *What the hell. The Rafkins are in jail. How can I get in trouble now? It's just research.*

Chapter 11

Sally had invited Susan for an early dinner, quickly preparing a salad to go with a couple of lamb chops. This would be their first working session.

"Tony suggested I look into the New York Mob's early days. Research is something I'm pretty good at," Susan said between bites of buttered bread. "If Mrs. Rafkin is ninety-six, she was born in 1926. What was her maiden name? Was she an only child? Was she groomed to be her father's successor? Who was her father and what was the extent of his Mob business connections?"

"I'll look into those businesses and numbers. Why don't I take Tony's advice and pretend to open each of these businesses, while keeping my fortune hidden from the IRS. It will be an interesting challenge, especially since we have no idea of the amount of money that would have to be laundered," Sally offered. "And using your timeline, where did the rich bank their fortunes?"

"Let's take this one step at a time. Since neither of us has written a book, why frighten ourselves by looking too far ahead. If we tackle this like a game, maybe it won't be so daunting," Susan offered. "Look, the Rafkins haven't even gone to trial. We have plenty of time."

"Damn the Rafkins. Lisa's book will be written," Sally said, her determined commitment to their project evident.

"I can't thank you enough, Sally. I was feeling so out of my depth, alone and needing to at least try to finish what Lisa had started."

"I mentioned before that I feel some responsibility as well. Seeing your name as coauthor with your niece on a finished book will be my reward."

Sally sipped her wine, lost in thought. What was she thinking? Year-end was her busiest season. *I've six clients depending on me. And with Jeanne roping me into family Christmas planning, research would have to take third place.* But she was committed. Never one to shirk a challenge gave her the focus she would need.

"Right and working together it might go even faster than we think," Sally said, and dishing out dinner, raised her glass. "To us. To success."

"I'll happily drink to that," Susan replied with a grin.

* * *

That night, Sally tossed and turned in bed, focused on money. *I know Tony said he would look into the money angle. But I can't get it out of my head. If I was a 1920s banker for the Mob, where would I hide the proceeds of the Gambino criminal endeavors?*

The dream took on another dimension, focusing on a news story where a reporter thought he had found Al Capone's safe buried in the cellar of an old building... then recalled it had been empty. *So, the size of the safe would indicate cash. But how much cash?*

Bleary-eyed, Sally walked into the bathroom, stepped into the shower, and after brushing her teeth, looked at her bedside clock on her way to the kitchen for a strong, mind-clearing cup of coffee. It was five a.m.

"Cash in cash out, no one to record the income for the government to find," Sally thought aloud. "But today we don't deal in cash. At least not in amounts that would require it to be hidden, so what were they doing that would earn large amounts of money? Those forged documents can't earn that kind of money. Diamonds? You would still need to sell them and then what would you do with the money?"

You're getting ahead of yourself. Think back in time.

OK, if cash became too cumbersome, you would bank it offshore. Switzerland? No, maybe after WWII that might have worked. But back in the twenties, it might have been Cuba. But these people are active today, so Cuba is out. With the IRS having made agreements with most of the free world to report US citizens' accounts of $10,000 or more, hiding cash will have changed as well.

After banks, maybe they exchanged cash for bearer bonds. But today, most all transactions of size are done electronically, so bearer bonds aren't as commonly available.

Drugs, like diamonds, could earn cash, again where would it be hidden?

That brings us to what the Rafkins were doing to require hiding large sums of money. The bookstore didn't look all that profitable. Mrs. Rafkin and grandson Aiden weren't as richly dressed as her neighbor, the restaurant owner in his Zenga suits. Sally remembered that they didn't even own their apartments. Modest would be her description of the Rafkin family and business. *Now, why don't they own their apartments?*

Two cups of coffee later, she turned on her computer and opened a search into money laundering. The phrase seemed to have originated with the Mob opening laundromats to exchange their profits from their illegal enterprises into everyday accepted cash.

So it starts with the Mob. Interesting.

Chapter 12

It was seven in the morning and all her research and thinking about money had done was raise more questions than answers. In her own life, lack of sufficient funds to pay bills had driven her husband mad with worry. She always seemed to be able to function on whatever amount she earned at any one time. It was second nature to save for her future. Then she remembered her mother saying, "Money doesn't hug back."

The ringing phone jarred her fully awake. "Mm, hello?"

"Sally, it's me, Jace. Did I wake you?"

"Not really. I was up early. Couldn't sleep."

"It's Saturday and I was hoping I could encourage you to drive up to the country for the weekend. If we leave before the nine o'clock rush, we can have two full days of nature."

"Oh yes. Can you give me an hour?" With her heart pounding, Sally's thoughts turned to another evening in Jace's arms.

"Definitely, I'll bring coffee and a Danish."

Sally was just leaving the entrance of her building when Jace pulled up in his suburban. "I love a woman who is always on time," Jace said, leaning over and giving her a quick kiss on the cheek as she settled in the passenger seat.

"Is that just in case we've still got watchers wondering if this is part of your detective's cover?" she quipped. Then, looking into his eyes, all but melted.

She couldn't stop smiling after Jace planted another quick deep kiss on her lips. "Oh yes, Jace, you are just what I need." The look on his face reminded her that this was a man who not only turned her on, but seemed to treasure her as well.

The drive up went faster than Sally had remembered, listening to Jace's plans for their time at the cabin. "So, I've brought groceries for a full eggs and sausage breakfast, and how about grilling steaks and hamburgers for dinner?"

"Yum. And if you have the makings of a salad, or fruit, maybe I can add to those meals?" Sally said.

"Ryan said you were an excellent cook. And that salmon was superb," Jace said, giving her an appreciative wink. "When did you learn how?"

"I've always fiddled in the kitchen, but I guess I'm a foodie. I mean, I can taste the differences in ingredients in a dish and am able to duplicate most dishes I've had in a restaurant. If I had one wish, I'd like to travel and sample the foods of other countries."

"Well, here we are," Jace announced as he pulled into the driveway of the cabin. Once again, as he helped Sally from the car and reached in the back to get her overnight bag, he leaned in for a long, slow kiss.

"Mm. Traveling with you is a sensory experience," she murmured, and standing in front of the wood house with the front porch waiting for their arrival, Sally no longer felt a stranger. Her growing relationship with Jace and his sharing of this family place all made her feel welcome.

At sunset, settled on a back porch swing bundled against the winter cold, they snuggled and sipped cocktails. Sally relishing the peace. Moving even closer to Jace, her mind was temporarily empty of words, just filled with pictures of the glorious display of nature in the distance. Snug in her quilted jacket with muffler and mittened hands, the cocktail added an inner warmth while the red of the setting sun dipping low over the mountain ridge in the distance soothed her jangled brain.

Darkness and the cooling temperatures moved them inside. To Sally's surprise, Jace began to set up a well-used grill in the fireplace. "I thought when you said grill, you meant outdoors?"

"After the sun goes down, it gets cold pretty quickly. We might cook outdoors during the day, but evenings we cook in the fireplace."

"I never learned to cook over a grill. I'm an indoor cook," Sally said, watching Jace's preparations.

As Jace placed a few bricks of charcoal under the grate, he added a couple of sticks of kindling to help start the fire. "Once the charcoal turns gray, we'll be ready to sear the steaks," he said. Then, getting up, moved to the kitchen and began working on the corn, removing the silk and placing the ears into the sink filled with water to soak. "These go on the grate before the steaks. If you've never tasted grilled corn, this should be a real treat."

Leaning in for a quick kiss, Jace grinned. "OK, chef, your turn; I'll get the salad makings. Can you make a dressing with only vinegar and oil?"

She didn't need any prompting; pulling out a cutting board and picking up a knife, began to turn whole vegetables into a garden of color. Instead of using his vinegar, she took a lemon and made a vinaigrette with garlic and other dried ingredients found in a cabinet. Whisking completed, Sally dipped a piece of lettuce into the mixture and offered it to Jace. "Yum. You did all that with those few ingredients? You're handy to have around," he quipped, brushing her lips with a kiss.

Soft jazz was playing on the phonograph and the table was set for two, when Jace took Sally into his arms, gently pulling her close, and whispered that he loved her. Cherishing this gentle man's way of loving, Sally gave in to her feelings. With this man, nothing was rushed. He was all about sweet words and mind-numbing kisses.

The evening seemed to float on a cushion, food and conversation so very easy between them. With dishes left on the table, Jace stood, and held out his hand for hers. "Dessert?"

"Mm, lately that is my favorite course," Sally whispered as she rose and took his hand.

Jace put his arm around her shoulder as they walked to the bedroom. Standing at the foot of the large bed, he leaned in for her kiss. "I want time with you. Slow, sweet hours with nothing to distract us," he said, his voice filled with the warmth of love. Sally nodded, feeling Jace lift her sweater gently over her head. The cool air rushed over her nipples, and when they brushed against his naked torso, sent shivers over the rest of her skin. Feeling totally free, she unbuttoned his jeans, and leaning down, ran her tongue around his navel. It was gratifying to feel his skin react to her touch. Feeling him lift her by the shoulders, she whispered, "I love you, Jace. I'm no longer scared to feel it. Loving you makes it right."

"I'd wait for you if you still need time. But I can't tell you how happy you've made me and that we've found each other. It's been too long without being able to love. To care for someone more than myself," he whispered. With soft white sheets awaiting their coupling, he lifted Sally and, hugging her close in his arms, gently placed her on the bed.

Sally saw love, passion, and need in Jace's eyes and held out her arms. The magic she felt intensified as they began to connect hearts and bodies in passion.

* * *

It was Sunday morning and with breakfast eaten, Jace led Sally out the back door. "I want you to experience the effect simply walking around the grounds has on me. It helps me release all the tension of my job."

The ground had a dusting of snow, and as they sat on a rock again facing the surrounding mountains, Sally understood what Jace had been talking about. She wasn't focused on her clients' taxes or her search for information about the Rafkins. She felt younger. At peace. With the crisp winter air warmed by the sun, she was quite simply enjoying the sounds and scents of nature.

"Since it's warmed up to a comfortable forty-five degrees, let's take a walk," Jace said and smiled, seeing that he had a willing companion for something he loved to do. "I'll introduce you to my favorite spots near the cottage." Taking her gloved hand, he began a slow pace, during which he pointed out his favorite views, only a rare cabin visible in the forest of trees. Today, the mountains also wore a dusting of snow that sparkled in the sun.

As she stopped to take in the view, Sally looked up and saw that look she associated with Jace knowing something was on her mind and just waiting for her to speak. "Ah, I know you can't discuss the Rafkins, but ever since you took me to that market in the Bronx, and tried to introduce me to what it means to be an Italian family, I wondered if that was the normal way for Mob families?"

"Normal?" Jace asked quietly.

Sally stopped Jace with a hand on his arm. "I mean, I'm not asking for specifics about the Rafkins' background, but how the Mob treated one another. You know, blood family. I only know what I've seen in the movies. What is that expression? En familia?"

She smiled when she saw that Jace understood her curiosity and accepted her probing for information.

"Let's sit over here and I'll try to answer your questions." Once settled on a wooden bench, he took her hand and, with a quirky look, acknowledged her curiosity. "Well, family was both the normal unit of parents and children. But with those men, family was also reserved for their inner circle… men who did the bidding of the Capo, or Boss. A closed society, if you will."

"And their businesses were profitable?"

Laughing, Jace leaned down and kissed her firmly on the mouth. It was more a kiss of approval than passion. "How can someone as smart as you, who has lived with this murder investigation for almost a year, still be so innocent?"

"I don't understand." Sally's frown showed her confusion. "I know they made money, and how the mobsters made it. That isn't really my question."

"It was all about money and power. The Mob was ruthless in enforcing their rules whereby people paid for protection… not to be beaten or robbed, or have their businesses burned down. Liquor was not only purchased by patrons of the speakeasies, but by the Westies, the Irish Mob on the west side of Manhattan, and even by the Tongs in Chinatown. Then there was the gambling and the sex trade. Are you beginning to see that Mrs. Rafkin comes from a violent lineage?"

"Money. How much money? Amounts that needed to be laundered and kept from the eyes of the government?"

"I've heard that one of the capos pulled in twelve million dollars a week from the liquor trade alone." Not hearing anything, Jace looked over and saw Sally was stunned by the information. "Twelve million in 1920 would be billions today," he added.

"I am beginning to see why Lisa was so fascinated by this story. But Mrs. Rafkin could be living a larger life if she had that kind of wealth. Something else must be involved," Sally murmured, thinking that even if she couldn't verify the exact extent of the Rafkin's fortune, she had some inkling of its magnitude. Sally was aware of Jace's sudden scrutiny. *He knows what I'm thinking.*

"Sally, I know this sounds like fun. Please believe me that you must be careful. Keep whatever you find to yourself. And, yes, I must be kept informed of the leads you follow and who you speak with. Even with the Rafkins in jail, they still have underlings reporting to them. If you are found asking questions, they might place you under surveillance." *I can't tell him that I had a feeling someone was watching me at the memorial. He'd go ballistic.*

"Sweetheart. Listen carefully," Jace said, needing to get her attention. "Lisa Clark was killed for looking into those dark corners of the Rafkins world."

Moving to his side, Sally whispered, "I promise to let you know what I find. Even the people I speak to." Feeling Jace's arms around her, Sally silently vowed she would.

Chapter 13

Sally and Susan walked into the Gramercy Park Hotel bar, which looked like a setting from the Gilded Age, with planted palm trees separating settees and tables strategically located around the room. Tony Granger stood and waved them over to a table in the back of the lounge.

With drinks ordered, Tony sat back and smiled. "Well, ladies. I have a contact who must remain anonymous, but owes me a favor, so has agreed to talk with you."

"That's wonderful," Susan replied calmly. She trusted Tony, having known him for ten years.

"Fabulous," Sally chimed in a bit more enthusiastically.

"We'll do a video chat tomorrow. I've arranged for my publisher to lend us the library. All nice and private. I thought we might go over the questions you have before then."

"Money. How much? Millions? Billions? Where did they hide it?" Sally was breathless from rushing to get it all out. She wasn't expecting to see a frown on Tony's normally calm face.

"Could we be more specific?" he asked with all the patience of someone accustomed to interviewing subjects for one of his books.

"Of course," Susan replied. "The information we found so far was cryptic and limited. My niece was going to look into the Gambino family of the twenties. Also any political influence they may have had in the city."

"Another thing, Tony," Sally began. "She also had a list of names of businesses, but we told you that already. And so far, I haven't been able to find any information on them. So are they domestic? Foreign? Is there a directory of businesses not on the Stock Exchange? I mean those under private ownership? What about secret banking connections?"

"Yes, follow the money," Tony quietly answered, and looked as if, while expected, it wasn't what he had hoped to hear.

* * *

"Ladies, before we move over to the desk and log into the private session, I must insist that I ask all the questions. Your presence was demanded to verify that I wasn't the one seeking information for a book. Unfortunately, this person doesn't think very highly of women. So be patient and write me a note if there is anything I may have missed."

Well, back to being an empty-headed female. "Fine. That makes sense," Sally said, hiding her disgust.

"Susan?" Tony asked next.

"I agree, Tony. We will do as you ask. Especially since you are sharing one of your underworld contacts with us," Susan added.

The tea tray set up on the table in front of a sofa and two side chairs reminded Sally that this would be the kind of business setting she hoped to have in the future. Drapes set off the leather upholstery of a deep forest green, and that color was woven into the oriental carpet covering the seating area. But looking at her watch, she realized they wouldn't have time to enjoy it.

The man on the computer screen was in shadow. If Sally were to guess by his voice alone, she would have placed him in his sixties. Not only because it was graveled, but the vocabulary was out of a 1940s gangster film... youse guys, capo, connected, rat, and squeal.

"So, my friends are researching a book about the old days and wondered where the capos kept their fortunes," Tony asked, as if it wasn't really all that important.

Sally wondered why Tony was being so matter-of-fact. She doubted the man on the computer monitor even knew how to be subtle.

"You mean from the business? Not what they put back into the operations?" The question asked after a few moments of silence.

"I've heard stories that Al Capone, after being released from prison where he served eleven years for tax evasion, couldn't remember where he hid his millions due to syphilis," Tony volunteered.

"Yea. So? Dutch Schultz took his fortune of cash and treasure and hid it somewhere in the Catskills. People are still trying to find it." The gruff laughter that followed stunned Sally. How could losing a fortune be funny?

"I can't believe that all those fortunes didn't find their way to the families," Tony said. "Wouldn't the men have wanted to take care of their wives and children?"

"There's the family and business. Families had their homes and the legitimate incomes that the capos paid taxes on. They did very well."

"Can you give us some idea of how much these businesses earned... or where it was kept? If it was millions back then, it'd be worth billions today."

Suddenly the man chomped down on his cigar and, with a scowl, reached for his keyboard. "We're done here. I want to watch my grandchildren grow up." And with that, the connection was cut.

Sally was fuming. "The bastard. How could he just cut us off?" she all but yelled at Tony, while Susan, an observing Catholic, was crossing herself for protection.

Tony just shook his head. "Ladies, I think you should stop this research right now. I don't want to be an alarmist, but I didn't expect his warning. I'll help you craft a book. However, if you value your life and mine, you won't dig into this family or their ill-gotten gains."

"Warning?" Sally asked. "He just hung up."

"Yes, and said he wanted to live to see his grandchildren grow up. He wanted to live," Tony shot back.

"We understand," Susan said, not concealing her fear.

Sally sat mute. All of the warnings she had from Jace and Ryan didn't cause her the same sense of fear as this one incident. Then she remembered her meeting with Jace's FBI contact. What was his name? Tom something. He had warned her as well. *Don't be ridiculous. The murderous Rafkins can't touch me now that they are in jail.*

Chapter 14

The day was half over as Sally left Susan with Tony and walked home. *She's so comfortable with him, maybe she can get the name of another one of his contacts.*

Fresh air and the honking of horns helped keep her mind off her fears. She had accepted concern for her safety by Jace and Ryan. They loved her. But this warning from Tony Granger was different. It raised chills. *Shit! He apparently has an in with all sorts of underworld characters. His books keep selling… and he's still alive!*

The question was, did she want to continue with this project or drop it and return to her safe life? Hadn't she more than enough excitement in the past year? Now that she had regained her sense of independence with newfound love, an expanded family, and a growing business, did she want to jeopardize that by angering the wrong people?

Remembering that it was Jeanne's day off, Sally clicked on her cell and punched in Jeanne's number. *She'll help me sort through this dilemma.*

"Hey, girlfriend. Care to join me for a cappuccino over at that diner near you?" Sally said, hoping her tone didn't broadcast her dilemma.

"Sure. I'll bring our shopping list. Remember, you're going to help me shop for Christmas gifts."

"Right. See you in ten minutes or so. I'm walking, so it might be a bit longer." Hanging up, Sally headed uptown. The diner was only five blocks up and one avenue over. On automatic, her mind kept replaying Tony's warning to stop their research. *Hell, I will.*

* * *

"Thanks for meeting me like this. I needed a hug," Sally began.

"If I know you, it's a lot more serious than that," Jeanne replied, hugging her best friend and promptly leading her inside to a booth separated from other tables.

"OK. Spill it. Don't leave anything out," Jeanne ordered.

Why did she always finger silverware before speaking? Jeanne would keep her secrets. "OK. Remember I mentioned that Lisa Clark's aunt, Susan, has asked me to help her finish that book her niece was working on?"

"The one Jace and Ryan aren't too happy about?" Jeanne's disapproval was evident by her tone.

As Sally nodded, her frown deepened. "Has Ryan mentioned it to you?"

"Of course. He's worried sick about you. We both know when you get an idea you don't let it go. But this isn't like signing a new client. You're talking about raising the dead."

"Well, not exactly. It's more like trying to trace a lot of money."

"Can you give me some idea of why, and how much we're talking about?" Jeanne's skepticism colored the tone of her voice.

Just then, a waitress stopped by the table to take their orders. Jeanne, quick to continue her conversation with Sally, piped up, "Two cappuccinos and biscotti. Thanks."

"And?" Jeanne said, returning to focus on her best friend. Having lived with Sally prior to her marriage to Tyler, Jeanne could read her expressions as if they were printed on her friend's forehead. Even though Christmas was two weeks away, shopping could wait.

"So Susan introduced me to Tony Granger, one of my favorite mystery authors. He offered to help us with the book."

"Why would she do that? And how does she know him?"

"Susan used to be the executive assistant to a senior editor at Tony's publisher and has worked with him since he signed with the company some ten years ago." Looking away, she hesitated, lost in an inner battle of how much to share with Jeanne.

"And...?" Jeanne asked somewhat impatiently.

"And she asked if he might be able to help us research the book. Her thought was that since he was known for writing about crime, including characters modeled after the murderous Mob of the 1920s, he could help us with our research."

"Sounds reasonable. Or was it?"

"It was. But…"

"But something happened to gum up the works?" Jeanne prodded.

Nodding, Sally added sugar to her coffee that had just been placed on the table. Stirring the beverage seemed to stiffen her resolve. "He set up a video chat with a man who he thought would answer some of our questions. We weren't given his name and he was kept in shadow, hidden so we'd not be able to identify him."

"He was going to tell you where to research the Mob?" Jeanne's voice filled with dread.

"No. Tony had asked us what we wanted him to tell us. Jeanne, believe me, it was all about the money. Where the fortunes of these mobsters had been kept. That sort of thing."

"You are sitting here telling me about some video chat with a mobster that Tony felt was perfectly safe?" Jeanne leaned forward and grasped Sally's hand with a firm squeeze. "Sally, I've known you for years and you don't look like you feel safe."

A single tear slipped from Sally's eye as she collapsed back in her seat. "And when this guy asked us what we wanted to know, Tony calmly said that we were interested in finding out what the men did with their fortunes. And how much money was involved. He just cut the connection. Even Tony was stunned. After gathering his thoughts, Tony warned us not to continue with our research."

"Whew. When you get involved with something it's never boring."

All Sally could do was agree. *I shouldn't have bothered Jeanne. It's my own fault.*

"What are you going to do? Ryan and Jace would tell you to take his advice."

"But I can't. I found Lisa's body. I was involved with the investigation into her murder. Jeanne, these neighbors of mine didn't look like mobsters. It was an old woman and her grandson. But they are… or at least descendants of mobsters. I just want to help finish Lisa's investigation into money laundering. I'm not trying to dig up someone's grave."

Sally's plea for understanding made Jeanne consider just what she should advise. "Are you asking whether or not you should continue with your research? Or stop now while you and Susan are ahead?"

"Yes. It sounds so simple when you say it."

"I'm not sure how I can help. But knowing you, you won't let it go. So I will speak to Ryan and at the least, maybe he can find a way for you to do your research safely."

Chapter 15

Ryan suggested Jace meet him at a bar on the corner of his block. Since it was out of the detective's usual territory, he hoped it would shield them from prying eyes. Over the past several weeks, Ryan's respect for Jace had grown, knowing that in loving Sally, Jace would do anything to see her safe.

The two men sat hunched over the table, lost in thought. "Damn it, Ryan," Jace all but exploded. "I can't keep Sally away from writing that book… even though the information she and Susan turned up only suggests this family's financial machinations. But money laundering has become her new favorite phrase. She knows I can't talk about the Rafkins or the status of the trial, but she keeps asking about broader topics like describing the Mob meaning of family. And that is even more frightening."

"I know. She's focused on finding the money earned by the old woman's father."

"You're her brother-in-law. Can't you talk to her? She has a business with a respected list of clients, a stable home and, finally, a new relationship with me. How can someone so accomplished be so clueless?"

Looking into the tortured man's face, Ryan just shook his head. "Jace, you saved her from herself. This book has brought the woman I first met back to life. Not just the book. You, Jace, brought my sister-in-law back to the loving woman who married my brother." Looking at the frustrated man, Ryan didn't think he had heard one word.

Jace brought his drink to his lips and put the glass down without a sip. "How can I keep her safe? She tells me it's her responsibility because she found Lisa's body. Doesn't she get it? These people are murderers. She could get killed!" Anguish permeated the air around both men.

"Okay, Jace. This is what we have to do. Jeanne will get Sally involved in Christmas for the family so she doesn't have any free time to continue her research. You, my good man, will dazzle her by continuing to show her parts of New York, making her feel settled... I hope."

"Will Jeanne continue to share Sally's activities with you? So we can know what she's up to?"

"Of course. She's as worried as we are. I called you because she came running to me yesterday after seeing Sally. Apparently, that Tony Granger set up a video chat with some gangster and he cut them off. Jeanne was totally beside herself with fear when Sally told her that Tony had warned both women to stop working on Lisa's book."

"OK. I'm going to get in touch with my friend at the FBI and off the record see if he has turned up anything. I promise to stay in touch."

Hoisting his glass of beer, Ryan said, "A deal."

Chapter 16

"Jeanne, I just can't drop everything to go Christmas shopping. It's end-of-year tax time. It's also when I draw up a schedule of recommendations for my client's consideration to expand or streamline their businesses."

"Christmas is family. And we are your family," Jeanne cajoled.

Sally knew Jeanne was right. The research, not family, was keeping her from her accounting responsibilities. Looking at the phone, she took a deep breath. "When and where do you want to meet? I'll give you one day this week; you just take me around the stores. OK? Will that make you happy?"

"Absolutely. And knowing you, who in leaner times sewed special outfits so your step kids could look as well dressed as their friends at the country club, shopping for them will bring you back to happier times. So, meet me at ten at Macy's. No excuses."

* * *

The main floor of Macy's New York flagship store was crowded with customers jammed on escalators headed for the upper floors. The main floor was decorated for the Christmas holidays and people looking for a particular department rushed past Sally, who stood still in amazement. She had been raised with suburban shopping centers where department stores were spread out. Not like this behemoth rising eight floors in a building set on a full city block. Now looking at the flow of mostly women, some with small children in tow, she began to get an idea of just how intensely people outside her small world lived.

"Wow, Jeanne. How do you know where to go?" Sally said in wonder.

"This is usually my first stop now that Lord and Taylor and Bonwit Teller are no longer with us," Jeanne replied, then turned and saw Sally's bewildered look.

"You mean there are more stores like this?"

Jeanne realized just how sheltered her friend's life had been. There was nothing like the intensity of being in the midst of Christmas shopping in a mega-sized store famous for its Christmas windows. Chuckling, Jeanne quipped, "This is a city where anything and everything can be found at almost any price. Now let's start with Judy and Jane. OK?"

"Oh yes. I'd love to buy each of the girls a dress." Seeing the horror on Jeanne's face stopped her in her tracks. "What?"

"May I recommend not a dress, but maybe an outfit. Jeans, sparkly top, and hoodie. Things they can wear together or separately but not look like paper dolls."

"Oh, Jeanne, I've lost touch. I wouldn't want to embarrass them. Please, just show me what you mean."

The areas on the floor Jeanne led them to were separated into sections, each featuring a designer brand. Finding a selection with age-appropriate separates, Sally began to pull together a coordinated look. "Jeanne, I know Judy liked pink, but maybe now something a bit more her age, like maroon. Here's a pair of designer jeans and matching maroon long-sleeved t-shirt with embroidery and glitter. What do you think?"

"Great idea, and I'll select the same styles but in Jane's favorite color blue."

It took an hour more to select shoes and a puffy vest to go with each of the girl's new outfits. "Sally, look for backpacks in coordinating colors," Jeanne called out.

After paying for their purchases, Jeanne suggested, "Come on, we can go to the restaurant for a light bite and coffee. On me." Jeanne was smiling as she led Sally to the elevators for their trip to the basement.

With scraps of pastry left on their places, Sally looked at her watch horrified to find that it was almost four. "Jeanne, look at the time. And we haven't done the boys."

Secretly thrilled by Sally's acceptance of the diversion, Jeanne was hesitant to over-schedule future excursions. "And I have to work tomorrow. Why not meet up Friday and we can take care of the boys… the big and small ones."

"But Friday I was going to go to the New York Business Library for some research," Sally replied.

"Christmas is almost here. Can't you put your research off until the new year?" Jeanne asked wistfully.

"Of course. Organization of all those to-do things on your list. It's just that I've never done a full Christmas with kids and grownups… and wish Jace could join us." Perking up, Sally looked to Jeanne with a smile and a renewed spirit of fun. "Yes, Christmas must be done right. I'm all in."

Jeanne was delighted to see Sally absorbing her expanding world. What was it that Barbara confided when they were last together? *Sally just needed time to find herself.*

Chapter 17

Fidgety and unable to wait for Tom to arrive at seven, Jace sat at a back table of the neighborhood bar nursing a scotch. All he wanted to do was wrap Sally up in a blanket and carry her off to the cabin. Turn off all phone and internet services, get a large dog for company, and protect her from unknown assailants. Taking a sip, Jace decided he was being too melodramatic.

While they had been friends ever since they joined the police force, after two years, Tom moved over to the FBI. He said he needed a wider field in which to investigate all manner of crimes. Not wanting to take advantage of their friendship, Jace had only once contacted his buddy for support and that was the Lisa Clark murder investigation. With that solved, Jace's interests returned to the local police department's demands of too few detectives to handle increasing incidents of crime in the city.

"You look old," Tom greeted him, setting a glass on the table and pulling out a chair opposite the distraught man.

"I feel old. Tired. At my wits' end," Jace replied, hoisting his glass and reaching over to clink it with Tom's.

"It can't be work. You thrive on murder and mayhem. It must be that pretty blonde you introduced me to."

"How did you get so smart? And, yes, it's Sally. What do you remember about her?"

"Obviously pretty, certainly smart, and very observant. That tie clip clue was unexpected."

Jace looked at his friend and nodded as he slumped back in his chair.

"And you were obviously besotted with the little lady," Tom added with a smile.

"Besotted? Where did you come up with that one?"

"Since I've known you, Jace Logan, you have always taken murderers and other criminals in stride. So when I see a crack in that composure, it must be personal," Tom replied with a laugh. "I'm guessing that this time, your investigation into a group of very bad characters is threatening your lady friend."

"It's about 'those characters,'" Jace began.

"I'm listening, pal. Tell me what you need."

"That lady is now my girlfriend, and one of her most maddening traits is her curiosity."

"Hey… Jace in love. What the devil took you so long?" Tom raised his glass in silent toast, and took a quick sip. "She's perfect for you."

Silence followed Tom's comments, clearly in favor of Jace and Sally's budding romance. "Yeah. She's kind, sweet, and loving. Imagine a vision in looks and brains who cooks."

"You didn't bring me out in this cold to fill me in on your love life." Tom's serious tone reminded Jace why he called.

"No. If you remember my case was to find the person or persons who murdered that young investigative reporter, Lisa Clark." Seeing he had Tom's full attention, continued, "Well, the young woman was killed because she had been investigating the Rafkin family and was going to write an exposé on the family's money laundering activities. Lisa Clark's aunt lives in Sally's building and they've become friends. My problem is that the aunt has asked Sally to finish the book her niece was killed for."

"Aren't the old woman, her son, and grandson in custody awaiting trial?"

"Yes. But my instincts are telling me that there is more to this little gang than those three. And if I'm right, when Sally begins digging into the Rafkins' finances, they are going to find out and stop her." Relieved to have explained his dilemma, Jace signaled for another round of drinks.

"Unfortunately, that isn't as far-fetched as you think. We've been keeping that house on Long Island under surveillance and believe the Rafkins were smuggling people into the country. And, if we're right, they've been doing it for decades, maybe back as far as the late thirties."

"Smuggling people? Why? Oh, wait. The old lady's son was arrested for forgery. Before we got into World War II, that would include spies, Nazis, and the German American Bund, not only criminals. They could have earned a small fortune by not only arranging for their transportation, but providing legal documents that enabled them to move around this country undetected."

"Your little murder is turning into a Mob family operation. And that seemingly quiet old woman is the daughter of a gangster. His only child," Tom added.

"And with Daddy's other activities, she is sitting on a fortune worth billions," Jace added. "Enough to be quite adept at laundering money." Jace, looking miserable, felt the danger to Sally increasing. "Tom, what do I do?"

"Does Sally keep you informed of her research? Maybe you can find a way to redirect her research to safer avenues?"

"Actually, it isn't just Sally. The aunt and Sally searched the reporter's apartment. They found a safe deposit key and memory card. Yes, Sally knows she has to turn what they find over to us. And bless her heart she has. She still doesn't know what's in the safe deposit box. They are waiting for the aunt to be officially named as executor of the estate."

"Anything on that memory card? Jace, this could be important." Tom's urgency was clear.

"Yes, but limited. It was a listing of names of companies… that so far Sally hasn't been able to track and I haven't had time to follow up on."

"OK. This is what we can do. Send me a copy of that memory card with the list of companies and I will fill you in on any progress on that smuggling operation."

"And Sally?" Jace pleaded.

"Stay close. She trusts you so maybe she'll be happy to share any new details her research turns up."

Both men downed their fresh drinks and rose with each focused on the evening's revelations.

Chapter 18

Adjusting the collar of her suit jacket, Susan gave her appearance one more look, from the collar of her silk blouse to her Gucci low-heeled shoes. *A trip uptown in slacks and a sweater? Unthinkable.* She was on a mission... researching Mrs. Rafkin's family at the New York Historical Society. As she picked up the calfskin folio, she caressed the soft leather and smiled, remembering that it had been a gift from Harvey, her boss at the publishing house. He had always been generous at Christmas, with little trinkets from Tiffany & Co., but this was to thank her for twenty-five years as his right hand. Lying on the desk were her tools: legal pad, pens, pencil, and tablet. With each item inserted in the folds and pockets of the folio, she grabbed her handbag and headed out the door.

The streets were busy with morning traffic, people bundled against the cold, rushing to their various appointments and jobs. *Just like the old days when I was one of them.* Deep in thought, the noise of traffic, and honking horns and sirens fell on deaf ears.

The bus ride across town didn't take long and gave her a chance to formulate a plan. Research was one of her skills. This time not for an author or business plan... it was to find out as much as she could about the people who murdered her niece.

At the information desk, she was directed to a table of computers and given instructions on how to access the ancestry programs as well as additional resources, including shipping manifests of immigrants arriving at Ellis Island, and census reports going back more than a century.

Ancestry. Was Rafkin the family name? Was she the matriarch? Did she have siblings, not just the one son and grandson?

"Oh, not really," she uttered. "Your married name was Rafferty. And you were only sixteen when you married." Changing her search to Rafferty, she found that the husband had died in a shooting three years into the marriage. "Married at sixteen, widowed at nineteen. So let's assume you got pregnant during your first year. Why did you change your last name?"

Further searches found that Lorenza was the only child of Alfonse Gambino. "The mobster?" A search of Alfonse found he was a cousin of Joseph Gambino, feared head of the Five Families, who were the notorious Italian clan active in New York City going back more than a century.

Stunned by the connection to the gangsters of the past, Susan removed her tablet and carefully entered the dates of births and deaths, and family connections to Mrs. Rafkin. Next, she'd construct a family tree and try to figure out a time frame that might lead them to any income, hidden or acquired.

I know Sally's concentrating on money; why don't I see if there is anything in the library about family fortunes. Susan approached the librarian. "Ms., do you have any records about wealthy families in the late twenties? Maybe those not accepted as members of the upper crust, but people wealthy enough to be newsworthy?"

Directed to several newspapers of the day, Susan thought someone had been following her from the computers to the newspaper files. *Identifying Mrs. Rafkin's family is making me paranoid. Then again, she comes from evil stock.*

Starting with the year 1926, she began to read about banking, the newly instituted income tax, and something called the Curb-market.

Now that is interesting. The New York Stock Exchange, founded in 1817, was closed to all but select members, trading stocks of established companies. But New York also had a burgeoning trade in companies transporting goods by ship, train, and over land. These were being financed by men standing on the street, and not being accepted into the Exchange, they sent young boys into the building to finalize the buy and sell orders. This became known as the Curb-market, and in 1921 was formalized as the American Stock Exchange.

That must have been a wild time. I must ask Tony about this. But I doubt the Rafkins would want people knowing about their business interests or family finances. I'm missing something.

As she continued reading the daily news, Susan began to worry that she had been naive. After reading page after page of murder, prostitution, robberies, and street killings, she wondered how anyone survived.

Sending a text to Sally saying that they had to meet, she pulled her jacket closer, suddenly no longer comfortable in the library. *I'm beginning to understand why that man cut our interview so abruptly and why Tony warned us away from our research.*

Packing up her things, Susan's mind wandered to scenes from gangster movies she had loved watching on television. *No. They can't be that brutal. After all, Lisa told me she was looking for a hidden fortune. Next on my list is to look into each of these men. Who were they? What part did they play in Mrs. Rafkin's life? Sally might know where I can look next.*

The vibration of her cell jarred her out of her thoughts. Checking the screen saw that Sally suggested she stop by at four and texted a quick confirmation. *Good. This should get us started, but after I tell Sally about that family, she might agree with Tony and not continue helping me with the book.*

Chapter 19

No time to think about what Susan had discovered. She'd find out when they met at four. Sally returned her attention to her reports, reminded that they had to be completed next week.

She was pleased to see that annual figures for Southern Comfort showed a year-end increase in sales. She could foresee Indigo hiring extra help so she could do what she loved best, create new recipes for her growing business. Maybe she would consider instituting a delivery service. Sally decided to check into the services she could use, and compare them to the costs of hiring her own delivery van. The graphics would be great advertising. Adding a few notes to her report, she closed out the file.

"Hello, Indigo?" Sally said when the cheerful young woman answered her phone. "Could we have a quick meeting after tomorrow morning's rush?"

"You sound happy; will it be good news?" Indigo replied.

"Yes, and I may have an interesting idea for next year."

"Okay. I'll make sure to have your favorite butterscotch nuggets ready."

On opening the file for Germaine Maison, Sally's attention was diverted by the ringing of her cell. "Damn it," she griped, calming down on hearing Jeanne's sarcastic greeting. "So when are you going to teach me how to make Christmas stockings? I was going to knit them, but that could take us into next Christmas. And we are only one week away from the festivities."

"What a friend you've turned out to be," Sally replied. "You know I'm busy and you call me away from year-end reports to help you make Christmas stockings?" she said, knowing it was futile to refuse. She loved all four kids, not just Tyler's son and daughter. Of course she'd help Jeanne with her holiday plans.

"What a nice addition to her store-bought presents," Sally cheerfully added. "Now let me get back to work."

* * *

Promptly at four, Sally opened the door and saw that Susan's normally pristine tailored appearance was marred by an unbuttoned jacket and loosened collar of her blouse. "You look like you could use a glass of wine?" Seeing a grateful smile, ushered her friend toward the kitchen. Opening the refrigerator, Sally pulled out a bottle of Sauvignon Blanc and poured two glasses, handing one to the unsettled woman.

"What's got you so upset? I thought you were going to do some preliminary research on the Rafkins?"

Nodding and taking a long sip from her glass, Susan looked up, clearly troubled. "I did."

"You visited the Historical Society?"

"Yes. And I copied the facts. Just basics about that woman's family."

"Then why are you so upset? It isn't as if you were interviewing some live person. It's computers," Sally said in a warm voice she hoped would help settle the clearly rattled Susan.

"Do you realize who this family is?" Susan began. "Think. If Mrs. Rafkin is almost one hundred, who were her parents, more specifically her father?"

"I guess he was Italian because her first name is Lorenza, and that isn't a modern name in any nationality. So?"

"Sally, she's Mob royalty." Susan's voice filled with dread.

"He wasn't one of those Five Family bosses. My early reading didn't include Rafkin."

"Sally, she married an Irish cop named Rafferty when she was sixteen. It is just possible that it was an arranged marriage since he died a couple of years later. When she was left with a son, she opened the bookstore—"

"And changed her name to Rafkin, to hide her family from scrutiny," Sally concluded in hushed tones. As she looked into Susan's eyes, it hit her. "Geeze, we're talking the 1920s Murder Incorporated. Not some local criminal family."

Sitting down, the room echoed in silence. Neither of them wanted to go any further. Sally needed to do something with her hands. She had gotten into the habit of snacking along with an evening glass of wine. Moving to the refrigerator, she pulled out an assortment of cheeses and salami slices, automatically setting up a tray. Sitting the tray on the counter along with small plates and napkins, she refilled the empty glasses and finally sat down.

"That's what Tony's contact was referring to when he said he wanted to live to see his grandchildren grow up." Sally's tone echoed the danger they were facing. "He was warning us away."

"Lisa was murdered to keep that family's secrets. She may have thought it was about hiding an old fortune. In reality, she would have been exposing a criminal enterprise still in operation," Susan said.

"Susan, I don't mean to scare you even more, but I have to ask… do get the feeling that you are being followed?"

"Not really followed. More like being watched. Why?"

"Good. Because I've had that feeling before. It was months ago, after I left a meeting with Jace and a man from the FBI. Now, even though the Rafkins are in jail, I wonder if they have people who could be watching us?" Sipping her wine, Sally bit into a piece of cheese. "No, Jace would have told me I had been followed. Though he does continue to warm me to stick to research."

"We haven't done anything. You've done all your research online. I only went to the Historical Society today. Who would know we were looking into the Rafkins?" Susan whispered, afraid that if Sally had been followed, maybe they were on some watch list set up by the old woman.

"I think we have to meet with Jace before we go any further. Agreed?"

Susan expelled a deep breath, nodding her consent.

"It's toward the end of the day; I'll try him at the office." Almost as soon as she entered Jace's cell number, he picked up. "Sally? Are you all right?"

"Ah, yes," she replied, clearly surprised by his concern. "Would you be able to stop by to meet with Susan and me? We need to run something by you." Sally nodded to Susan, affirming Jace's agreement. "Great. I'll make a salad. Dinner and conversation," she continued, purposefully keeping her tone light. Placing the phone on the counter, Sally could hear all those months of warnings. Jace trying to tell her to be careful without successfully describing the people she was looking into. The simple finishing of Lisa's book had become a potentially life-threatening event.

Chapter 20

When Sally opened the door one hour later, she saw that she hadn't fooled Jace. A deep frown was etched on his forehead, and instead of his usual hug and kiss greeting, he steered her over to the sofa where a silent Susan sat waiting.

"Ladies, I do believe you have gotten into something way over your head. So fess up."

Sally got up and began to walk slowly around the living room, stopping by the carafe of coffee set out on a side table and poured Jace a cup. Without looking directly at him, knowing he could probably read her mind, she handed him the cup and sat in a nearby club chair. It wasn't the time for the closeness of lovers.

"Susan visited the New York Historical Society earlier today. Just to see what information she could find on the Rafkin family. Up to now, we... had only searched Lisa's apartment, which you already know about. And then I've tried to locate information about those company names on the memory card... which you also know about."

"Yes," he said, setting his coffee on the table in front of the sofa. "Leaving anything out?" Jace's penetrating stare had both women's full attention.

"And Tony Granger, the famous author of thrillers is a client of my old firm and he…" A cough stopped Susan briefly, then rushing on she said, "And I called him to see if he would meet with us." Finished, she clasped both hands tightly.

Jace, still quiet, kept his attention focused on both women. "And…?" His question didn't hide his displeasure.

"And, he's one of my favorite mystery novelists," Sally rushed in to save Susan further explanation. "We thought learning how he plotted a mystery might help Susan and me with this book."

"I can see that that isn't all." Jace's stern voice, while controlled, demanded they come clean.

"Well, he set up a video chat with a contact. We don't know his name and his face was hidden. But when we asked about money and where a member of the Mob may have hidden it, he shut us down," Susan blurted out without taking a breath.

"And you two then had to continue to look into this questionable family." It wasn't a summation, it was alarm. "So who are the Rafkins?" he asked, wanting to know just how much information these two innocents had uncovered about a family he was only too familiar with.

"Well, Mrs. Lorenza Rafkin was married to an Irish cop named Rafferty at the age of sixteen. He died three years later when she changed her name and opened Rafkin and Sons Antiquarian Books."

"Yes, Susan. So?"

Sally couldn't lie to Jace. "So her father was a Gambino," she blurted out.

"Now you see why I didn't want you to continue with this insane idea of completing Lisa's book?" Jace hadn't raised his voice but his anger did what Susan's research hadn't; it scared them.

"But, Jace, where's the harm? It isn't as if we spoke to anyone," Sally pleaded.

"That video chat, remember?" Jace had all he could do not to scream. "Do you think he couldn't identify you two?" Glaring at Sally, he shook his head. "Look, you must stop whatever you are doing."

Looking contrite, Susan looked over to Jace. "There's still the matter of Lisa's safe deposit box. We promised we'd tell you when I can open it... so you could join us at the bank." Her soft voice was shaking.

Jace just sat there. Sally could see the wheels spinning with conflict. "We might not find anything," Sally added as if an afterthought. "All we found were notes, nothing to uncover Lisa's overall theory about what and how they hid money." That didn't get the results she had hoped for. Jace was drumming his fingers on the arm of the sofa, trying to stay calm.

"Will you two promise me not to go any further with this insane idea until we see what's in that safe deposit box? You must swear to me to stop whatever you have planned until then. After that, we can see where things stand." Jace hadn't issued his request quietly, but with the firm voice of a seasoned detective facing two clueless witnesses in a murder investigation.

Dinner was clearly out of the question when Jace rose and, with a sad nod of his head, left the women to their personal thoughts.

Chapter 21

Would she ever sleep again? Where was that soft-spoken, kind man she'd fallen in love with?

It was four in the morning and her bed sheets were in a tangle. With sleep evading her every attempt, Sally crawled out of bed and into a hot shower. Scrubbing her head to clean its thoughts almost worked, but on emerging and drying off with a large bath towel, her brain once again kicked into high gear.

Well, one thing I know for sure, I don't know how to write a goddamn book. Booting up her computer, she looked for a writing workshop and found one that promised to help people start their books. *Great. A weekend program. Shit, I can't tell anyone what I'm working on. And according to the course description, you have to read passages to the rest of the group.*

"Hell, I can do a weekend, but how would I do the required work?" The ringing phone jarred her fully awake.

"Sally, you promised to spend the day with me to shop for gifts. I'll pick you up at ten. Okay?" Jeanne's happy voice echoed in her ear.

"Uh huh. Ten is fine. See you then," she replied, not looking forward to a day with her nosy sister-in-law/best friend.

Jeanne was surely going to question her about Jace and what she and Susan were up to.

* * *

Opening the front door to her townhouse, Jeanne dumped her packages on a nearby table. "Everyone's out, so it's just us. I'll get the wine, take off your coat, and meet me in the kitchen," Jeanne ordered.

"Yes, ma'am," Sally quipped.

Taking a glass of her favorite white wine from Jeanne, Sally waited for the questioning to begin. Her problem was just how honest to be. If she scared Jeanne, Ryan would call Jace and they would have a meeting about stopping the book. *I can't let that happen.*

"You know, Jeanne, since COVID, all those little boutique-like shops have closed. Shopping isn't as much fun. I feel guilty just buying the kids' stuff. Store-bought t-shirts and jeans for Judy and Jane, and manly fleece jackets for Billy and Mark," Sally said.

"Those jackets for the boys have their favorite New York Yankee logos. They are going to love them," Jeanne said.

"Yes. And the outfits for the girls are really fun and a brand they seem to talk about. But I used to sew things for the kids. It isn't the same."

"I know what you mean. But aren't you giving the kids those scrapbooks made with Tyler's photos taken in Antarctica?"

105

"Absolutely, and that gives me an idea. You are going to make Christmas stockings for the whole family," Sally said and, glancing at the petrified look, laughed.

"Don't look scared, you won't need my sewing machine… just felt and glue and some ribbon. We'll go to the hobby store. They may even have kits." Sally's smile was contagious, and Jeanne found herself smiling back.

"Tomorrow, and I'll pick you up at the same time. The kids can go to a friend's house and Ryan will be at the office. We can get what we need, come back here, and make Christmas stockings for everyone, then hang them up before anyone comes home," Jeanne said.

"Done and now I have to go home," Sally said, getting up and grabbing her coat. Not waiting for Jeanne to change the topic and probe into her personal life, she hugged her friend and made a quick exit.

Chapter 22

Sally and Barbara had no sooner rung Ryan's doorbell on Christmas Day when four excited children opened the door and, laughing, pulled both women inside. The entryway was trimmed in ribbons of evergreen hanging from over the entryway into each room. Single candles lit window sills and soft choral music played throughout the home.

"Aunt Sally," Mark said, spotting the large suitcase she was pulling behind her.

Hugging her nephew close, Sally announced, "Gram and I stopped off at the North Pole and Santa asked us to deliver this to you."

With the yelling of excited children following Mark to the Christmas tree, he unzipped the case and began handing beautifully wrapped packages to his sister and cousins for placement around the tree. At the bottom of the case were four identically wrapped square packages.

With her face wreathed in smiles, Sally removed all four gifts and, walking toward the children, began handing one to each. "These are from Tyler and myself."

The silence was brief, but at the mention of Billy and Judy's dad, everyone stopped what they were doing. It wasn't the reaction Sally had hoped for, but looking at Billy and Judy, knew that the loss of their father was still fresh. And admittedly, even after five years, it still caused her pain.

On opening her gift, Judy's fingers caressed the cover photo of her smiling dad. A tear fell and looking to her brother saw he too was teary-eyed. Leaning down, she whispered, "Billy, when I graduate high school in three years, I'm going to get a job and an apartment. You're going to move in with me." Billy nodded. "I'll get a job too." With a brief hug, they began looking through their book of photos taken in Antarctica.

"This is a happy gift, kids," Sally said, trying to lighten the mood. "Uncle Ryan gave your dad a special camera, Billy. He used it to capture photos of our trip to the White World so you could not only see what we saw, but know that there is a magical place on earth where penguins play, whales swim, and seals sun on aqua-tinted ice."

As Ryan took their coats, he leaned down and kissed Sally on the cheek. "Thank you," he said, barely hiding his tears. Hugging Barbara, he turned to his wife, knowing she would re-energize the group.

"Enough for now, kids. Let's eat our holiday feast, then open the rest of your presents," Jeanne said. When everyone was settled at the table, Ryan stood. "This is a time to remember those no longer with us with love and know they remain in our hearts. And love those here today. Family all. Amen."

The quiet voices echoed similar feelings.

"Jeanne, you have outdone yourself," Barbara said as she cut into her roast beef. "I must say that the last time I made a roast was when my husband was alive. It was his favorite dish."

"Mine too, Gram," Billy chimed in.

It warmed Sally's heart to see her mom so well accepted. She'd been a widow too long and having grandchildren to love had her blooming with happiness.

Table talk by the kids was all about guessing what Barbara and Sally had brought. Jeanne and Ryan were delighted to have the family all together and not dealing with grief, dangerous research projects, or the fact that after New Year's Day, Billy and Judy would have to go back home.

Two hours later, with a tangle of torn wrapping paper and untied ribbons stuffed into a plastic bag, Ryan handed around cups of hot chocolate with marshmallows. "Why not take your gifts to the den, kids?" Ryan said and was pleased that they didn't have to patiently listen to the excited kids go over each and every item with their parents looking on.

"Ryan, you have something to say?" Sally asked, getting a strong feeling that this gathering had a special meaning for him.

Nodding yes, he set down his mug. "Sally, Jeanne and I have been talking about Billy and Judy having to live in that loveless house with a woman who treats them as prisoners. What would you say if we adopted them? They'd keep the Scott name, and could visit with you whenever they wanted." Looking at Barbara, he saw approval and love.

Barbara reached over and hugged her daughter close; silent tears were streaming down her face. "Ryan, anything I can do to assist, please ask. I love those children and they would not only have a loving home, but cousins to share school and friends with."

"If only that could be so! But Victoria would want the earth and moon from you, thinking that you were wealthy and an easy touch. She'd play her wounded wife role. *That woman stole my husband and now you want to take my kids away from me?*"

"Maybe. But just maybe if she kept receiving their child support as defined in Tyler's will, without the bother of her growing son and daughter, I could convince her to give up what she has always thought of as impediments to her personal life."

Jeanne returned from checking on the kids, who were all involved with their gifts, and found a silent and somber group of adults. "What's this? It's Christmas," she said, trying to lighten the somber mood.

"You are absolutely right. Christmas. A time for joy." Sally's cheerfulness brought back the holiday spirit. Grateful for the love from Ryan and Jeanne, that they would try to save Billy and Judy from their uncaring mother, reached deep into her heart. They were giving her a precious gift. *This is the loving family I've always wanted.*

Chapter 23

Ryan and Jace were huddled at a corner table at Neary's on 57th Street. They had arrived at four, Jace leaving work early, and Ryan having told Jeanne he'd be home after six. Unlike the local bars they frequented, everyone who visited Neary's, regardless of the time of day, was greeted like family.

"Nice change," Jace remarked, feeling that everything must be under control as Ryan seemed relaxed. "You a regular? They seem to know you."

"Yes. A favorite. We could do a date night here. Simple menu and friendly crowd," Ryan suggested. "By the way, we missed you at Christmas."

"I missed all of you as well. Was it noisy? Too many gifts for the kids?" Jace's wishful expression was welcomed by Ryan, who already felt he was family.

"You know, Ryan, I've hesitated in asking, but Tyler. You know I love Sally, but sometimes I feel that shadow of your brother's presence. Maybe you could clue me in? I'm not asking for family secrets, just to know their relationship. Was it like mine with Sally? Different?" Jace wasn't prying, he just felt that even in death, Tyler was competition.

Smiling, Ryan sat back. "My younger brother was guilty of only one thing. He loved Sally to distraction and, in doing so, bankrupted himself. Yet he wouldn't share that with her, fearing she'd stop loving him. You see, Sally worshipped Tyler. And, when he died in that accident, she quickly learned they were deep in debt. Even worse, he'd made sure she didn't get pregnant, afraid he couldn't pay the bills."

"Adored? We're more like two college kids finding lust and romance at a later stage in life."

"Sally is different now. No longer loving blindly. She sees you for who you are and loves as deeply, but I'd say on a more adult level. In the past four years, she's grown into her own. I wouldn't worry about the past. You and Tyler fell in love with different women."

Signaling for the waitress, Ryan asked, "What will you have? Beer? They have a good selection."

"Oh, whatever they have on tap is fine. You just set my mind at ease. Thank you. But I believe you have something on your mind." Jace's calm comment was greeted with a nod.

Ordering two draft beers, Ryan came to the point. "Jace, have you spoken with the prosecutor about a trial date? Maybe if that bunch is put away, Sally will be safe even if she continues to work on that damn book."

"The prosecutor says he has a strong case for murder one for the grandson, maybe a lighter sentence for the old woman, but the son's only provable crime is forgery. That is going to require a separate trial."

"Did he have any idea when the trial will start? The sooner this is over, the happier I'll be."

"Sometime next year, probably not before September. The court docket has a huge backlog of cases. The trick is to keep Sally and Susan off their *project* till it's over." Jace spat the words spat out with distaste.

"September? Not sooner?" Ryan's question was delivered in desperation.

"Sorry, pal. The wheels of justice… need oil," Jace added, trying to change the subject over which he had no control.

"Jace, isn't there still something about a safe deposit box?"

Jace grimaced. "You seem pretty well informed. Does Sally confide in you… when I've told her not to speak to anyone?" Then he cringed when he saw the hurt on Ryan's face. "Sorry, man. I know you wouldn't do anything that could hurt Sally. It's just that she's driving me crazy. And, the worst part is if it's known that we are seeing one another, her position as a witness for the prosecution will be tainted," Jace explained.

"So not only could someone hurt Sally, but if her testimony is thrown out… they could go free?" Jace's firm nod confirmed Ryan's alarm.

With the beers served, Ryan took a small sip and remained silent, deep in thought.

Jace had an idea that might solve both their problems… keeping Sally safe. "Don't you have Billy and Judy for the week? Now that Christmas is over and it's a few days before New Year, what if I invite Sally to have all of you join me up at my family's cabin? I can get a few days off. It would be fun."

It was as if he'd triggered a magic button. Ryan lit up with the first smile he'd seen since they entered the restaurant.

"Think of barbeque, toasting marshmallows in the fireplace… all that kind of stuff. The kids can use the sleds if it snows, and if not, there is a horse farm nearby. I even think the closet has puzzles and games we played as kids." Jace's excitement was contagious.

Raising his glass, Ryan toasted, "To Family, Fun, and Games."

Chapter 24

"Well, I'm worried that whatever my niece has saved will not be helpful in completing her book." Susan's remark broke the silence in the car. She had dressed as if for a funeral, in a tailored black suit and coat. Sally noticed only her firmly clenched jaw showed her tension.

"That's all?" Jace said, trying to keep his tone light and not jump down the older woman's throat.

They were heading for the bank to finally see what Lisa had hidden away in her safe deposit box. Neither Sally nor Susan wanted to confront Jace with their fears. Somehow, he had become their guide, steering them away from danger. But they didn't know what was to come. So far, what they had found on the memory card and in the notes hidden in Lisa's recipe books was vague and hadn't led them anywhere. Only Susan's research identifying the Rafkins as connected to the Mob of a century ago reminded them that Lisa had been fishing in dangerous waters.

"No, that's not all, Jace," Sally said, interrupting the silence. "We're petrified that she had a very good reason for her fascination with this unholy family." All three remained quiet as Jace continued driving. He was unable to disagree.

Entering the bank, Susan approached a teller. "May I help you?" the young man asked. The group's silence didn't seem to raise any alarm from the teller.

"Yes, young man. I'd like to check this safe deposit box." Handing him the papers naming her executor of Lisa Clark's estate, along with a copy of her niece's death certificate, she waited patiently for the young man to finish checking his computer terminal.

"Everything is in order, Mrs. Clark. Come with me," the pleasant late twenty-something man said as he led the group down two flights of stairs to the vault.

While Susan followed the bank clerk, Jace took hold of Sally's elbow and, with a slight squeeze, reminded her to stay silent.

"Mrs. Clark, if you will kindly give me your key, I'll get the box. You can use this room and lock the box in its place when through." With that, the man opened a small door in the wall of similar doors and withdrew a long black metal box. Handing it to Susan, he nodded and left the three alone.

"If you don't mind, I'd like to say a prayer before we open this box," Susan said. Closing her eyes, she mumbled, "Please, Lord, let us help Lisa complete her task."

Susan handed Jace the key. "I'm afraid I've waited so long to see what's been saved, I prefer you do the honors." Susan

ed aside and crossed her fingers, again closing her eyes to say a silent prayer.

As he opened the long box, they all peered in and saw a manila envelope. Withdrawing the envelope, Jace handed it to Susan.

Shaking it upside down, they watched as a small audio cassette dropped to the table. Reaching into the envelope, she next withdrew five typed pages with a small envelope clipped at the top and handed both to Jace.

"Susan, this envelope is addressed to you," Jace said, handing it back to her.

With shaky hands, Susan opened a three-by-two-inch folded note and recognized her niece's half printed, half scripted handwriting in her favorite green ink. *Dear Aunt Susan, if you are reading this, my curiosity has caught up with me. Please do not grieve because I honestly believe that when the proper authorities hear the tape and read these pages, justice will be served. It may be a century too late, but I will have facilitated the exposure of this notorious family and their multiple crimes against this country.*

"May I?" Sally asked Jace, reaching for the typed pages. She calmly skimmed the pages and, looking up, they saw she was amazed at what she had read. "Holy Mother of God." Realizing that Susan and Jace were waiting, Sally calmed herself. "I think we should leave and discuss this back at the apartment."

117

Jace packed up the tape and papers, enclosed them in the envelope, and handed it to Susan. He then replaced the empty tray in its place on the wall of similar boxes, locked it, and handed Susan the key.

The drive back to the apartment building was a somber one. Jace found a parking spot across from the entrance and followed Sally and Susan to the elevator. Entering Sally's apartment, Jace steeled himself for the next threat to both women. How could he continue to protect Sally and Susan from their heroic but reckless desire to finish Lisa Clark's exposé on the Rafkin family?

"Get settled. I'm going to get a bottle of wine and glasses. Then I'll give you the short synopsis of those pages, or read them if you prefer."

"So Lisa uncovered a smuggling scheme going back to before World War II," Susan said, having listened in amazement to Sally's recitation of the papers.

"More than that. Apparently, this is the personal testimony of Mrs. Rafkin's uncle, who spent his entire life as that old woman's babysitter and bodyguard. It says that his nephew gave Lisa this information because she promised to give his uncle credit for his devotion to his brother, Alfonso, and Lorenza, his daughter. The tape is his uncle's life in his own words and verifies the activities of the Alfonse Gambino family."

The silence that followed was of three minds absorbing the shock of not only the magnitude of what Lisa had led them to believe was simply a money laundering operation, but something even bigger. It was the history of a crime family protected by the famed Five Families… the Mob.

Not wanting to lessen the seriousness of this information, Jace pointed to the pages. "Sally, please make a copy for yourself and Susan, and I will have a duplicate made of this tape sent over to you."

Sally, lost in thought, took the pages to her copier and made a duplicate set. As he reached out for the originals, Jace stood, replaced the information in the envelope, and in his firmest, most direct manner said, "OK. I'm going to tell you both one more time, and having seen this information, you will agree that nothing can be done, even hinted at until the trial is over and the criminals are convicted. And even then, only when there are no appeals by the defense attorney."

"But, Jace." Sally's voice was rushed in alarm. "We haven't played the audio tape. We don't know what this man said, or how he's connected with the smuggling operation, or even if he knows where the family hid their fortune." She didn't like not knowing the rest of Lisa's information. Her frustration at being shut down was not lost on Jace.

"No, and for the moment, to protect you both from yourselves, I am going to take the tape, make you a copy"— he held his hand up to stop Sally interrupting him again—"and once I've heard it and shared it with Tom, I will have you visit the station and listen to it yourselves. Do I make myself clear?"

He should have been pleased to see two heads nod in agreement, but fearing that Sally's curiosity would make it hard for her to comply, pulled her to her feet and with a strong squeeze of her shoulders, gave her a stern look. "I just found you and have no intentions of exposing you to murder."

"Susan?" Jace continued, turning his attention to the woman sitting silently nearby. "Can I trust you not to speak to anyone at your office, especially the author who set up your *chat* with that mobster?" He relaxed his grip on Sally. Hearing Susan take a deep breath, he watched her nod. "I promise, Jace."

Turning at the door, he looked back, wondering if the message was clear. "Anyway, it will make a better book once the Rafkins are imprisoned."

All the oxygen in the room seemed to have left with Jace. Sally and Susan were immobile, trying to accept their increased danger.

"Susan, I need a drink! Sidecar?" Sally offered, getting up and heading for the kitchen. Seeing her nod in agreement, Sally disappeared and reappeared with a cocktail shaker and two glasses.

"Jace is right, Sally. Not that I like it. But with what I found out about that family, and now a summary of that tape, I think we must wait for the trial."

Sitting next to the chastened woman, Sally raised her glass. "May God keep score."

Susan crossed herself. "Amen."

Chapter 25

The Scotts and four kids, and Sally and Jace, arrived at the cabin in two cars brimming with laughter. As kids scrambled out and immediately ran to the cabin's front porch, Ryan and Jace unloaded overnight bags.

Even though it was hard for Sally to set aside her thoughts about the Rafkins, she was excited to be surrounded by family, and couldn't be happier that Jace was part of the merry group.

"OK, gang, grab your bags and follow me," Jace called out. Amid the scramble to get the right bag to the right person, Jeanne directed traffic, closed car doors and, taking her husband's hand, joined the noisy group as Jace opened the front door to the cabin.

"Oh, Jace," Jeanne gushed. "This is perfect. Imagine someone as civilized as you, living a reclusive life up here," she teased. His wink and sly smile let her know that he was no longer living a hermit's life.

"For that, you get to help Sally unpack the groceries," Jace ordered with a grin.

"Jace," Sally called out. "I spoke to Mom before we left and she is counting on us to join her for New Year's Eve. She reminded me that there is an annual fireworks show at the beach."

"Fireworks," Billy yelled, causing his sister and cousins to join in with happy cheers. "Will Gram still have her tree? I hope so. It will give Judy and me one more day of holiday."

Sally saw the sad look and caught Ryan's nod that he had overheard Billy as well. "Later," he whispered. She crossed her fingers that all four kids approved of Ryan and Jeanne adopting her stepson and daughter. They deserved to have a loving family.

With Sally and Jeanne setting up an assembly line for the kids to help make the salad and peel potatoes, and Jace setting the grate over a slow-burning fire waiting for the charcoal to reach the right temperature for grilling, Ryan washed his hands so he could make hamburger patties.

"Jace, we need some music," Jeanne said.

"Open the chest under the stairs. There's a whole entertainment setup. Have fun."

As the sun set, the happy group of children and adults, all bundled in winter coats, gathered on the back porch to watch the dramatic red and orange rays spread over the mountain range. The cold air was forgotten as all were captivated by Mother Nature's glorious display.

"Before we eat, I'd like to hold a family meeting," Ryan said after all coats were hung on pegs by the back door. "Let's sit around the fireplace for a cozy chat. OK?"

Knowing that nothing Ryan did would hurt, all gathered expectantly. Boys sat together on a bench, and girls next to each other cross-legged on the floor. Sally and Jeanne sat near Ryan, while Jace stood off to one side.

"Billy, Judy, how would you like for Jeanne and I to adopt you? Jane and Mark said they loved sharing their rooms with you and you wouldn't even have to change your names."

"But, Uncle Ryan, how? Mother won't let us out of her sight," Judy said, her frown etched deeply on her forehead.

"Well, before I talk to your dad's attorney, we needed to know if you would like to come live with us. Then you would attend the same school as Mark and Jane and get to know their friends. Wouldn't you like that?"

Judy walked over to Ryan and reached up to hug him close. Billy, close behind with a grin, received a hug of his own. "Is that a yes?" Ryan asked. "

"Yes, Yes, Yes," the two clearly delighted kids yelled.

Sally, with tears in her eyes, watched the hope and happiness of her stepchildren. Yes, she'd have her family, all of them together. If she couldn't adopt them, she could love them along with Ryan and Jeanne.

"Aunt Sally? Do you approve?" Judy asked, hope clearly reflected in her eyes.

Looking at Judy, then Billy, she gave them the biggest smile she had. "I've loved you two for years, and now we can be together whenever you want."

"What do you mean, Sally? We're adopting you as well," laughed Jeanne.

"Now you must promise not to say anything to your mother. And try not to look any differently than you normally do when you go home. It's important that she not know our plans until she meets with the lawyer. Understand?" Ryan asked.

"Anything, Uncle Ryan. We swear," both Billy and Judy said with fingers crossing their hearts.

Chapter 26

Barbara opened her front door wide and welcomed the crush of adults and kids all dressed in their holiday finest tucked under their winter coats. Joining them was Jace Logan, who Barbara had grown very fond of after she saw how he went out of his way to make sure that her daughter was safe... not only from that murderous family, but from her daughter's curiosity that even as a child would get her into trouble.

Reaching up to kiss Jace on the cheek, she was rewarded with a warm smile and a return of the same. "So, camping out at the cabin was the fun-filled time you all wanted?" she asked.

"Mrs. Compton, that cabin has been empty for too long. Your family reminds me of mine and enjoying the country with my two brothers. For two days, I was surrounded by laughing kids." With a wide grin added, "Not to mention your lovely daughter. And it looks like your home continues to hold all of us in loving arms."

Barbara hugged Jace closer, then turned her attention to the crowd waiting for her orders.

"OK, drop your things in the back room, wash up, and join me for dinner. I've tried to make favorites for everyone. Mac and cheese with bacon for Billy and Mark, hamburgers for Judy and Jane, lamb chops with cream spinach for Jeanne and Ryan, and steak and salad for Sally and Jace."

"Barbara, how do you remember everyone's favorite dishes?" Jeanne asked.

As she looked at her daughter's best friend, Barbara remembered all those years without hearing the laughter of a child. "I love those kids. That makes remembering their wishes and likes easy."

With the fragrance of home cooking surrounding the happy group. Barbara laughed when Mark yelled, "Wow, what a feast!" Heartfelt cheers and applause followed.

Jace noticed that each of the dishes was served in colorful Portuguese earthenware dishes. These were touches he noticed when he ate at Sally's, thinking that these two women showed love even in the serving of a meal. Living alone as he did, everything was chosen for practicality, not for the way it looked. *Sally, you've enriched my life in so many ways.*

"You look lovely, Mrs. Compton," Jace remarked as he passed her on the way to his place at the table and was delighted he was sitting next to Sally.

"Barbara, it was a wonderful idea for the men to wear tuxedos and the boys blazers. They look like proper gentlemen escorting their favorite gals," Jeanne said.

Sally was smoothing her perfectly fitted dress. "I never asked you, Jeanne, but these dresses were Christmas gifts.

How did you find just the right styles for Mom and me?" Sally asked, taking her seat.

"Your client, Megan, of course. She knows you both so well, even had them hemmed to the right length."

"Boys, don't all the ladies look lovely?" Ryan asked and was rewarded with yea's and smiles. Raising his glass of prosecco, he looked around the table. "To our family. To welcoming the new year with heartfelt love."

He always says the right thing, Sally thought. *Tyler would have been a bit more formal.*

"Mom, it looks like everyone is trying everything. You have outdone yourself." Sally's love was clear in every word.

The pecan cranberry pie was dished up in the kitchen and topped with a mound of homemade whipped cream. Jeanne and Sally served each plate. "Coffee, tea, and milk over there, just help yourselves," Barbara directed.

Later, with the dishes done and everyone sitting around the den, kids sprawled on the floor, and adults on upholstered sofa and chairs, Sally wondered what her stepchildren were thinking. *Are they wishing Tyler was here?*

"You know at midnight the tradition is to make a New Year's resolution. Something you hope to accomplish during the coming year," Sally began.

"Like an assignment?" Mark asked with a frown.

"No. Like going to the gym for me. Because I sit all day and exercise would be good for me," she replied with a laugh.

"Or not to snack at work," Jeanne said. "I've been putting on weight."

"On you, my love, it looks perfect," Ryan was quick to add, receiving a kiss in return.

"Let's go around and see what each person is wishing for in the new year," Sally said. "Ryan, why don't you go first."

"To spend more time with my family. Mark and Jane are growing so fast, they will be married before long. And I've missed too many years working."

Turning to Jeanne, Sally winked. "And you?"

"Ryan has already gotten me to reduce my hours at the hospital. I think I'd like to begin knitting again. And maybe Jane would join me. Then, next year, you will all get homemade presents."

"I'd try it if we could take lessons together," Jane said.

"Done and done," Jeanne said, throwing the girl a kiss.

The room clapped their approval.

Sally, seated next to Barbara, leaned over and gave her a hug. "Mom? What would you wish for?"

"As you know, I've never traveled. That was something your father and I were going to do after he retired. Some of my friends have been talking about taking a river cruise in Europe."

"What a great idea, Barbara. And if you enjoyed that, maybe sometime we could all take a trip together," Jeanne said.

"Billy? Judy?" Sally prompted.

Sally could see how close Tyler's children were by the way they looked to one another as if to read each other's minds.

"We talk a lot about how different Dad was after he married you. Before our mom and dad divorced, we would spend Saturdays with him. But those grew less due to his travel for work." Judy's sadness echoed in the room.

Billy then looked to Sally with all the seriousness of someone not accustomed to asking for anything. "When we spent Saturdays with you and Dad, he was happy. We had fun. And you showed us what love is." Sally moved over to sit next to him on the floor and wrapped him in her arms. "You and Judy are my children and there isn't anything I wouldn't do for either of you."

Nodding, Judy added, "Wish we could be with you all the time."

The room fell silent as unshed tears sparkled in Ryan's and Barbara's eyes. Sally's pleading look signaled Ryan to please do everything he could to make their adoption possible. She needed to remove her kids from Vicious Victoria's grasp. He nodded. After getting the children's approval the day before at the cabin, he had phoned his brother's attorney and instructed him to begin working on the kids' adoption.

"Jace, this is a tough mood to follow. Care to share your thoughts?" Ryan asked, breaking the silence in a cheerful voice.

"Yes. I too have spent too many years wrapped up in my work. I definitely plan to rectify that," he said with a wink directed toward Sally.

"Wait a minute," Jeanne said. "Sally, you haven't shared your wish. So what is it?"

With a mischievous grin, she looked to each and every one. "More of this. No matter where we are."

Laughter filled the room. "OK. Enough of this. Time for a game of charades. Pick your teams. Will it be boys against girls, or grownups against kids?" Ryan asked.

"Boys against girls," the kids yelled, and moved to be close to their teammates.

A noisy couple of hours later, all headed for the festivities dressed for the cold winter temperatures at the beach. "I've not been to New Year's Eve at the beach since Sally left home," Barbara said, giving her daughter a warm smile. "As I remember, the town puts on quite a show."

Joining the crowd already gathered on benches set up in an area next to the parking lot, a hush fell as the town mayor welcomed one and all to the annual firework celebration. Then, one by one, rockets and brightly lit flares lit up the sky. Each successive explosion of color and design more brilliant than the one before.

Jace pulled Sally into his arms and, kissing her cheek, whispered, "My New Year's resolution is to love you and your family." Sally snuggled her back to his chest and gave herself to the explosions above and those in her heart.

Chapter 27

The dinner dishes had been cleared and Sally, Susan, and Jace sat with coffee in silence. Conversation had been focused on family and the prior week at Jace's cabin, followed by New Year's Eve with Barbara in New Jersey. "Susan, the fireworks were wonderful, but the best was that I now have hope that Billy and Judy will be adopted by Ryan. They deserve to live a life meant for two wonderful children," Sally said.

Sally and Susan hadn't seen one another since Jace's last warning for them to stop researching Lisa's book. Now, back home once again, the project, as they had been calling it, was back on both women's minds.

"Right!" Jace said, breaking into the quietude. "By now you know that if I seek a dinner invitation with you both, I have something serious to discuss."

"We're all ears," Sally replied, knowing this lead-up meant Jace expected their full attention… and she suspected, cooperation.

"The prosecutor has moved the trial date to the beginning of June. I know you have been wondering why an arrest of a year ago hasn't been sent to trial before now. And the truth is that the federal court system is swamped. While the forgery case against Alfonse will be tried separately, Mrs. Rafkin and her grandson, Aiden, will be tried together for murder."

"I have to go to the trial," Sally blurted out, interrupting Jace in her excitement. "This unspeakable family has to be convicted."

Shaking his head, Jace held up his hand to stop her. "Sally. Let me finish, please."

"OK, but why are they now setting a trial date?"

"You are aware that Mrs. Rafkin had a severe stroke that left her paralyzed on the left side and with speech difficulties. The prosecutor pled special circumstances for someone with her medical condition and advanced age of ninety-seven. That her presence was critical to presenting his defense for the murder of Lisa Clark."

"Is the woman that ill?" Susan asked.

"Yes and no. I believe she has been hiding her recovery. Throughout her lockup in the medical wing of the prison, she has paid for a private duty nurse and physical therapist, which leads me to believe she is playacting."

"And why can't I go to the trial?" Sally's defiance echoed her displeasure.

"Because, my love, you may be called as a witness to the day and time you first spotted the body. And I don't want any spies in the courtroom to spot you. We've kept you safe with the made-up story of our having a relationship. But I'm certain that this family has associates out there who are ready to execute their nefarious bidding."

What Jace's opening comments hadn't done, his mention of people employed to do the Rafkins' bidding was unnerving. It reminded her just who these people were.

"Sally, don't worry. Remember, I was an executive assistant and take shorthand. I'll be in court every day taking notes. You can write them up every night. That way, you can keep an eye on the entire proceedings."

"Thank you, dear friend. And that may help us when this man allows us to finally finish Lisa's book." She couldn't help being a bit snippy. Looking up, she saw that Jace was waiting for another shoe to drop.

"OK, Jace. In the meantime, where is that copy of the audiotape you promised us?" Sally asked defiantly.

Jace, trying to keep his temper, and seeing that he wasn't going to avoid their request, nodded in recognition.

"Jace, all we want is what my niece left in her safe deposit box. That can't be against any of your rules," Susan said softly.

"I'll see what I can do. Promise to get back to you tomorrow at the latest," he said and rose to leave. "Thank you for dinner, Sally. Ladies, I appreciate your honesty and respect your desire for information. However, please follow my instructions to delay work on your project."

* * *

No sooner had he gotten behind the wheel of his car than Jace dialed Tom's cell. "We've got a little problem. Sally and Susan are asking to hear the tape."

"But they stopped their research?" Tom replied.

"Yes, for the moment. But they are pretty insistent."

"I have to play it for you first. Then you'll understand that this is an ongoing case. Somehow you will have to impress upon them that we are no longer just concerned about the outcome of the murder trial, but a scheme going back a century."

"I guess your investigation has proved fruitful. You can fill me in before the women arrive," Jace said.

"OK, be at my office at ten tomorrow and ask the ladies to be in my office at Federal Plaza at eleven. Maybe the official FBI offices will instill extra seriousness about what they will hear."

Chapter 28

The next morning, Jace, who was waiting by the entrance to FBI headquarters, met a severely dressed Sally and Susan, their pants suits in dark gray and black, and ushered them past the guard at the turnstile and over to the elevators. Arriving on the designated floor, Tom was there to greet them, then led them to a small office halfway down the main corridor.

"Ladies, please make yourself comfortable. I've set up a coffee urn on the table over there," he said, pointing to the side of the room.

Sally and Susan walked over to the table and filled paper cups with coffee, adding sugar and creamer from an assortment set out for their selection. "Thank you for seeing us on what must be short notice," Sally said in a pleasant voice, moving over to a seat at the long conference table.

Jace, though he remained silent, wasn't fooled. As sweet as she was, the love of his life had a steel-sharp mind. "Tom, why not let the ladies know what we discovered on the tape and why you haven't made them a copy."

"Right. As you know, Jace has closed his investigation on the murder of your niece, Mrs. Clark. However, the information your niece left behind is an interview with a relative of a man we have had under surveillance. This is a new development and has turned out to be a far more complex and long-standing situation. This interview was freely given by one Carmine Gambino, son of Mrs. Rafkin's uncle, her father's brother."

"Quite a family." Sally's sarcasm was not lost on the others. Tom saw Jace's raised eyebrow and knew he was reminding him not to be fooled by her seemingly conventional remark.

"To your point, Mrs. Scott, the papers actually describe a family under the leadership of Mrs. Rafkin, focused on smuggling and forgery. Not the extortion, sex trade, and gambling of her father."

"Smuggling? Yes, there was something about that in the summary papers," Susan remarked.

"According to this interview, it began before World War II, when people were smuggled into the United States, driven from Long Island to the brownstone on St. Mark's, given forged papers and clothes, allowing them to move about the country unobserved."

"Spies? Nazis?" Sally asked, her curiosity tinged with foreboding.

"Among others wanting to remain unnoticed by our government," Tom added and seeing them focused on his information, continued. "We currently have a man working undercover in the area. As of now, he's been friended by someone who is part of this Long Island operation. We do know that even though Mrs. Rafkin is in prison awaiting trial, the smuggling continues."

"So arrest them," Sally demanded. "Then it will be over."

"Not so fast. Our agent has not yet worked with this person. Until he does, we have no proof or details about the operation. Further, we can't tie it to the Rafkins, or know how much the family has amassed from their illegal operations."

Jace turned to Sally and Susan. "What we do have is their tax returns. Unfortunately, everything, every dollar, is accounted for. It shows their bookshop income, bank loans, expenses, and personal living expenses such as taxes on the brownstone that they own, and the two apartments that they rent. Nothing we've reviewed is illegal," Jace said.

"If you let Sally and I hear the tape, maybe we'll be able to discover additional avenues to research," Susan said thoughtfully.

Tom gave Jace a stern look, to which he just nodded, clearly uncomfortable. "Tom, they don't see any harm in writing this book. To them, they are just following the money."

Tom frowned, then gave both women a similar stern look. "Ladies, it isn't just 'follow the money.' Firstly, we don't have any proof they are hiding large sums. Secondly, we haven't observed or found evidence of this people-smuggling operation Mr. Gambino, who I remind you is no longer among the living, is referring to. Until we can follow our current lead, the tape must remain with the FBI to prevent any interference with our surveillance."

"Maybe I can explain our procedures, Tom," Jace said. Forcing calm, he looked first to Sally and then Susan. "You see, if we spook anyone mentioned by Mr. Gambino, we won't be able to stop the operation or keep you two safe. As Tom mentioned, the members of the organization led by Mrs. Rafkin go beyond her blood family."

"Sally, there is still the trial. Maybe by the time that's successfully over, the FBI will have the proof they need to get the rest of these criminals. Then we will probably have an entirely different book to write. Not money laundering as Lisa thought, but one family's business dealings going back a century. That might just make a stronger story," Susan said.

Looking over to Tom, Sally nodded in agreement. "I guess now there is no rush to finish the book." Clearly frustrated, Sally looked to Jace for some sort of encouragement. At the least, support.

Standing to signal the end of the meeting, Jace looked to Sally, then Susan. "Ladies, I must thank Tom for reading you in on this ongoing case. But I must also remind you that everything he's said must be kept to yourselves until he gives you permission to include it in the book. As I said before, our current focus is on sending the Rafkins to prison for murder. Tom's undercover operation may enable us to prosecute them with additional criminal charges at a later date. So we must make sure we don't hinder Tom's investigation. Am I clear?"

With silent agreement all around, Sally rose to shake Tom's hand. "Thank you again. I just wish we had more information."

Chapter 29

The warm June courtroom was set up with a jury of six men and six women, already questioned by lawyers for both the prosecution and defense. So far there wasn't anything untoward, thought Susan, who had been present during the juror selection process. Her skill with shorthand enabled her to capture the names and brief backgrounds of the final members of the jury. It was agreed that Susan would attend the trial and Sally, being forbidden to attend, would organize all information Susan captured in her daily notes of the proceedings.

In planning their coverage, Sally and Susan had made charts and lists to be filled in as the trial progressed. A corkboard purchased for the occasion sat propped up on a bookcase in Sally's living room. The excuse was that it would make writing the book easier, but in truth, Sally reminded Susan, her job was to gather information that Jace, in his official capacity, had not been authorized to share with them.

Susan was grateful for her education on federal trials from her boss, who had kept her involved with Tony Granger's manuscripts. He had answered her questions about jury selection and how to look for disconnect between the truth as we know it and lies. Now, she sat in a mid-row, ready to take notes. This wasn't just a trial of the guilty. This was personal. Her niece's murder would be avenged.

"Your Honor, we thank you for changing the schedule to permit this trial to go forward with the presence of Mrs. Lorenza Rafkin," began District Attorney George Randall, who would be prosecuting the case. "I will be presenting evidence that will prove beyond doubt that Mr. Aiden Rafkin, with the assistance of Mrs. Lorenza Rafkin, his grandmother, willfully trapped and murdered Lisa Clark."

From Susan's seat in the courtroom, she didn't have a visual of either the woman's or her grandson's facial expressions. There was nothing she could do about that but try to observe any overt behavior.

"Mr. Donner?" Judge Johnson called out to the defense attorney, Stanley Donner, to begin his opening statement.

"Yes, Your Honor. My clients, Mr. Aiden Rafkin and Mrs. Lorenza Rafkin, plead not guilty to the charges of first-degree murder. I will present evidence that will refute the prosecution's position and prove that these law-abiding citizens have done nothing to warrant these charges. In fact, the search of their homes was illegal, and conclusions of the prosecution invalid."

"Mr. Randall, you may begin," the judge said, with Susan noting the time and date the official presentation of arguments began.

"For my first witness, I call Detective Jace Logan to the stand." Susan watched Jace approach the bench, looking composed. This wasn't the man she had come to like and look on as a friend. His almost military posture, dressed plainly in a dark gray suit, white shirt, and plain tie, was that of a professional detective and ready to respond to the attorney's questioning.

"Will you please recount your introduction to the murdered woman, and how you proceeded with your investigation."

As Susan listened carefully, she realized that it was Sally who had unknowingly provided Jace with important leads. It gave her a new insight into her friend's capability for observation of seemingly small details. Susan remembered Sally telling her that she felt responsible for having inadvertently spotted Lisa in the elevator of their apartment building. That finding her killer had become important, a personal commitment.

"And once you examined the scene with Ms. Clark's body, what were your next steps?" Randall prompted.

"There was no identification on the body, and the doorman on duty didn't know who she was, so the first step was to identify the victim. My partner began ringing doorbells and showing a photo of the young woman to building residents and staff alike, to see if anyone knew her. I spoke to the doorman, asking why he had called the precinct. He said that a resident had alerted him that something was amiss in the elevator, and on his checking the building camera, saw the victim lying on the floor."

As Susan took notes, she remembered speaking to Jace's partner and the shock of identifying her niece's body. Wiping at a tear that threatened, she focused on capturing all she could of Jace's testimony. But during a break in questioning, while the DA consulted with a colleague, she looked at others in the courtroom and noticed a strange man sitting in the back row. He stood out because instead of business dress, he looked like a tradesman taking a break from his job. He had weathered skin and wore a short-sleeved shirt that showed a pair of hairy burly arms. *I must be overstressed to think this man's looking at me.* Shaking her head, she turned a page, ready to continue recording the balance of Jace's testimony.

* * *

Later, with court adjourned for the day, Susan arrived at Sally's where she promptly accepted a glass of wine. "Well, it's begun. My notes will just tell you what we already know, Jace following up on examining Lisa's body and gathering whatever evidence they found in the elevator and on her body."

"I hope this is a slam dunk. That the trial won't last more than one week. After all, they have the DNA connecting Aiden's to Lisa's body," Sally said.

"Maybe. But there was a man in the courtroom that just looked odd, like someone who knew the Rafkins. I don't know, he was just strange and I thought he was watching me."

"No one knows anything about you. I don't suppose you could photograph him, if he's at the trial tomorrow?" Sally asked.

"No cameras allowed. You know that, Sally. We could alert Jace, though."

Sally picked up her cell and punched Jace's private number. "Jace, Susan thought someone in the courtroom was watching her. She didn't recognize him." Listening and nodding, Sally felt better for having checked in with Jace.

"Jace just said he'd have someone in the courtroom tomorrow and see if that man is in their files. If so, he will stop by with several photos for you to look at."

"Thanks. It's probably just my imagination," Susan replied, and reassured, took a sip of her wine.

* * *

The following day, Susan watched Dina Wagner, Lisa's editor, take the stand. From what her niece had said about her job, this woman left her to write pretty much whatever she wished.

"...so Ms. Wagner, you assigned Ms. Clark the stories you wanted her to report on," continued District Attorney George Randall.

"At first... When she started at the newspaper. But after she had handed in a couple of articles, I asked her to submit a list of stories she would like to cover."

"Do you always give your reporters freedom to choose their stories?"

"Not at all. However, Lisa wrote a monthly column in which she profiled a small business. Her talent was in making those people and their business so attractive that our readers wanted to visit them."

"And did they?" The DA's question was promptly answered.

"Not only did they, but our circulation grew with each and every profile she wrote."

"Now to the reason we are here. Did you suggest that Ms. Clark profile Rafkin and Sons Antiquarian Books?"

"No. It was on a list of possible profiles she had handed in. However, she told me that she had visited the bookstore and while they were polite and gave her a brief tour of the main floor, they were adamant that they did not want to be profiled."

"I see. Even, if as you have mentioned about other businesses Lisa wrote about, it would attract customers?"

"She said that their reaction to that was they had a clientele that wished to remain private."

"No more questions, Ms. Wagner."

Dina Wagner was the last witness for the day and as Susan packed up her pad and pen, looked to the rest of the courtroom audience, spotting that same man she had seen the day before.

* * *

It was later, at Sally's reviewing the day at court, when Jace arrived.

"This is a pleasant surprise," Sally said, ready for a kiss. "Or is it?"

Walking over to Susan, Jace opened an envelope and handed her six photos. "That man you noticed in the courtroom yesterday; do you see him in any of these photos?"

Picking up one, she showed it to Jace. With a smile, he nodded. "Sally, I'll take a glass of wine if you have one," he said.

Lifting the glass Sally had placed in his hand, he smiled again. "Ladies, that man is one of ours. So relax. Everything is as it should be."

Chapter 30

The corkboard was filling up with details. One page had a list of jurors. Another held Susan's transcribed notes for each day of the trial. And a third section of the board had a summary of the prosecutor's facts as presented.

"Susan, do the jurors look normal? I mean, do they look pressured? Like they might not be totally objective?" Sally asked.

"You've watched too many television trials. You can't be thinking that the Rafkins have pressured someone to cause a mistrial, or worse, not believe the evidence showing them guilty of murder," Susan replied, dismissing Sally's fears.

"Jace warned us off researching Lisa's book. I've started reading up on the actions of the gangsters from the twenties. They were an extended family tied by an oath of loyalty. A leader and soldiers set up like a military organization. So, if that was then, what about now? We have a woman raised in that culture. Like Tom said, she probably has her own team of henchmen doing her bidding. And just because Jace hasn't been able to find out how or where their money is, doesn't mean they aren't still earning it illegally." Sally was clearly on a roll.

What the intensity of Sally's previous statement hadn't done, she now had Susan's attention. "OK, Sally. Let's assume the Rafkins are today's Mob family. And the old woman is its leader. She sells books. Her son forges documents; that's pretty small time. Nothing like gambling, extortion, or rackets. So what would she be up to?" Walking up to the corkboard, Susan pointed to the Rafkin family tree. "Maybe we could go into the life of her uncle a bit further. Being older, he may have been the one who helped set up that people-smuggling ring."

Standing next to Susan, Sally added Al's name to the family tree. "We have to take Tom's information into account, not just post information from the trial. Her son was forging documents. That would be a direct connection to Tom's Long Island operation and the man his agent is following," Sally surmised. "Remember me telling you of that first meeting with Tom Stone? He was extremely interested in a man his partner had seen following me. I asked Jace about it, but he said he hadn't heard anything more from Tom. We now know Tom stayed with it."

"That was over a year ago. Did you believe him?"

"Yes, at the time. But now, it looks like that is the same man who led Tom to the Long Island operation. So Jace got his murderer. Now Tom is continuing to investigate whatever else that family was up to. Let's assume Tom's right and it's people smuggling," Sally said.

"I wish we had listened to that blasted tape. Maybe we'd have heard something that they didn't," Susan spat out in frustration.

"I'm going to push Jace to arrange for us to do just that," Sally swore.

"You know we need another list. A family tree for Mrs. Rafkin's father... we know her immediate family. And start one for the man on this tape. Maybe they are connected in a larger way than we first suspected." Susan's words caused Sally to nod in approval.

"It looks like the Rafkins/Gambinos are like an Italian Hydra, a many-headed monster," Sally remarked, crossing her fingers at the thought.

Chapter 31

With the DA not needing him for the fourth day of the trial, Jace's mind was swimming in unrelated questions and all circled back to keeping Sally safe. He missed her. Not the witness, but his love. Keeping Sally from herself had become a frightening challenge. She had no idea of what evil was. She'd simply classify this mobbed-up family as bad.

Sally, Sally, it's taken me all my adult life to find someone as sweet and loving as you. Please take my advice and stop work on that damn book.

Clearing his head, Jace walked into the local bar that became a favorite meeting place with Tom. Being ten minutes early gave him a chance to organize the questions he needed Tom to answer. It was their usual exchange of information, all outside official channels. He was ready to address any Tom might have regarding the murder investigation, especially if it helped his FBI task force look into the as-yet-to-be-proved smuggling operation.

"Thanks for meeting me, Tom. I'm hoping you would give me an update on your end of this Rafkin family situation. Sally is pressing me for a copy of that audiotape." Jace's tone was all business.

Throwing his coat on the table, Tom took a chair and, turning it around, straddled it. Signaling the waitress, he asked, "A Guinness for me," and seeing agreement from Jace, added, "and for my friend. Thanks."

"Trouble in paradise?" Tom quipped.

"No. Just keeping my two lives separate," Jace answered with a grin.

With the beers set before them, Jace took a sip of his. "Those notes and tape, are they helping your undercover agent get closer to your suspect out in Bayville?"

Tom, placing his elbows on the table, gave Jace a very direct look. "We tracked down the nephew mentioned on that tape. Apparently, this Sonny Carola is seventy. But with no photo ID, prison record, or employment history, we have no idea who he is or how Ms. Clark got the tape."

"How did you find him?" Jace leaned forward, not wanting to miss a word.

"The envelope you turned over to me had a return address and this Carola's name printed on it. It turns out that he is the old geezer on Long Island we identified from a photo our agent took last year." Tom, seeing Jace's questioning look, quickly added, "Remember I told you Sam spotted a man following Sally after our meeting. Well, he followed that car. Eventually, he led him to this man." Reaching into a briefcase, Tom pulled out the envelope and handed it over to Jace.

"Ah. So this is Sonny Carola," Jace replied, noting that he looked normal. Bulky for a man of seventy, with a clean shaved head. But then, what had he expected? Horns?

Moving his beer aside, Jace replaced the photo in the envelope. "And he gave the tape and summary pages to Lisa Clark? Why?"

"Maybe she promised to include him in a book about the Rafkins? Maybe she fed his ego as someone of importance to his family?" Tom answered.

"Have you spoken to him?" Jace's questioning look was rewarded.

"One of my undercover guys who looks about the same age met up with this guy in his local bar in Bayville. He said he was a driver for some local resident and after taking him home from the city, would stop by for a beer. They sort of became acquaintances. I haven't pushed him to find out anymore yet. I needed a plan. Something you are really good at, Jace."

Jace got up and went to the bar, and ordered two more beers and hamburgers. Bringing the drinks back to the table, he sat, removed his jacket, and rolled up his sleeves. "Didn't you say this geezer lived in an old wooden building right on the water? Like some summer cottage dating back to the thirties?"

"Yup. There are still a few left," Tom answered.

"If I were smuggling liquor, I'd want to have a boat available to go out to the clipper ships and unload the cargo.

And you are now thinking that after prohibition ended, people smuggling became the family's new cargo?" Jace asked.

"What else would be profitable? I doubt it would be drugs," Tom said.

"So if your undercover guy has established a relationship, maybe he could ask this Carola if he knew how he could earn extra money. That this driving gig took a chunk of time early in the morning and after work, but left him free to pick up additional jobs."

Tom slapped the table hard enough to cause Jace to jump back in his seat. "Now that's a plan!"

Chapter 32

Stanley Donner, the defense attorney, was sorting through files laid out on the table before him. Aiden Rafkin sat to his immediate right, and at the end of the table sat Mrs. Lorenza Rafkin in a wheelchair with a nurse standing just behind her. Both grandson and grandmother were in black. Subdued expressions, but eyes alert to every word spoken.

At the table for the prosecution sat District Attorney George Randall, and his associate, with files set out before each.

It was the second day and Susan's seat in the courtroom gave her a better view of the prisoners, and prayed once again that justice would be served and her niece's killers sent to prison.

"The defense calls Detective Jace Logan to the stand."

Jace stood tall as he approached the court clerk and was reminded that he was still under oath. Susan noted that he continued to look professionally alert, but then this wasn't a new experience for him.

"Detective Logan, how long have you been an officer at your precinct?"

"Just over six years."

"In all that time, have you ever arrested someone for murder?"

"Yes."

"How many times?"

"Unfortunately, about a dozen."

"About? Is your memory so bad you don't recall people sent to jail on your evidence?"

"No, sir. It is twelve. Each case was properly tried and in all, the perpetrators sent to jail." Jace remained calm, not falling into the attorney's trap.

Susan watched as Donner tried to smear Jace's reputation and record of presenting thoroughly prepared cases for trial. Now she knew how the defense would proceed in spite of the fact that there was DNA proof that the grandson killed Lisa. *Character assassination!*

With her pencil racing over her notebook as she tried to keep up with the testimony, Susan's head snapped up when Donner remarked that the main DNA sample was damaged and not admissible. It had been taken from skin found under Lisa's fingernails. *How in the hell?* Her attention was now on the attorney, not on her notes.

"Your Honor," said District Attorney George Randall. "I haven't seen the evidence that the defense is claiming inconclusive. I would like to request a recess until tomorrow to study a report including the chain of evidence."

"You have until nine tomorrow, Mr. Randall."

Susan watched the attorneys and their clients rise as the judge departed. *Tampering with evidence? Sally might have been right to think the defense would pull something.*

Arriving home earlier than expected, Susan called Sally's cell. "Your hunch that something hinky might be pulled was right. The defense attorney claimed critical DNA had been compromised."

"Maybe there's other evidence. I can't believe this case is dependent on only the DNA from under Lisa's fingernail."

* * *

With the jury in their place and the courtroom filled with almost the same spectators as the previous day of the trial, Susan once again noticed a man in outdoor wear and sunglasses in the back row, and relaxed remembering that Jace had said he was there to protect her. Settled, she turned her attention back to Jace and the beginning of his second round of questioning.

"Detective Logan, as mentioned yesterday, your case seems to rest on DNA evidence. Is that right?" asked the defense attorney, Sam Donner.

"Not entirely."

"The DNA was listed as primary in the papers the court provided me to defend my clients. Can you explain?"

"What evidence have you found compromised?"

"Well, the skin sample found under the dead woman's fingernails. Since you have no eyewitness to her death, that appears to be your only evidence that my clients were somehow involved in her death."

"There was additional DNA found at the scene of the crime. To my understanding, that is under lock and key at the precinct."

"The crime scene? Please explain."

"Evidence found in Mrs. Rafkin's apartment contained DNA evidence of bodily fluids from Lisa Clark, along with a blood sample of Aiden Rafkin. That linked him to her death and the location of her murder."

Susan's pencil stilled on hearing Jace's news. She wasn't alone, as she heard whispering from someone in the audience. This was something she hadn't known about and made a mental note to follow up with Sally.

Donner stepped back to the table and reviewed his notes, then stood upright and faced the judge. "Your Honor, I have no more questions for this witness." Quickly returning to his seat at the table, the attorney showed no reaction to this dramatic damage to his case.

"District Attorney Randall. Are you prepared to present your summation?"

"Yes, your Honor."

Leaving his file folder with notes on the table, George Randall walked to the jury and smiled. It wasn't an expression of happiness, rather one of empathy for the importance of their upcoming decision. Randall hoped his summation would clearly show Aiden Rafkin and the old woman were responsible for Ms. Clark's murder.

"Ladies and gentlemen, we have the responsibility of seeing that the death of Lisa Clark doesn't go unpunished. According to her editor, she was a bright light and had a promising future as an investigative journalist. Since she isn't here to speak for herself, we must review the actions leading up to her death and of those responsible.

"We have presented film taken from the elevator in which Ms. Clark's body was found and earlier footage that shows her going from her aunt's apartment on the fifth floor to the fifteenth, but never leaving the building.

"We have collected bodily fluids that would have been released at the time of her death. That sample included DNA from one Aiden Rafkin. This proves that the body had been moved from Mrs. Rafkin's apartment to the elevator, where she was found.

"It has been suggested by the investigators that when Ms. Clark had originally visited the Rafkin and Sons Antiquarian Book Shop, to see if she might do a profile of the firm for her newspaper, she was shown the door. We aren't sure what made her look into the Rafkins' business and family, but it had been mentioned to her aunt and a friend that she was working on an exposé about the Rafkin family who she believed to be engaged in a major money laundering scheme." George Randall had been walking slowly back and forth along the jury and at each portion of his presentation, made eye contact with one of the jurors.

"But this trial isn't about any business interests of the Rafkin family. It is to see that the murder of a young woman doesn't go unpunished. I thank you for your careful review of the facts of this case and seeing that the murderers of Lisa Clark never harm another person as long as they live."

Susan thought Randall had summarized the case clearly and in a tone of voice that spoke of integrity, not showboating.

"Mr. Donner. Will you present your summation to the jury."

"Yes, your Honor."

Unlike the District Attorney, Stanley Donner stood with a folder of notes in his hand, and seemed to strut toward the jury. Dapper, but a bit on the loud side with heavy satin tie and enormous gold tie clip, the only other sign of ego was his slicked back hair.

"Ladies and gentlemen of the jury. What we have here is a case of mistaken identity. We are saddened to learn of the death of Ms. Lisa Clark. However, as the prosecution has already mentioned, my clients did not work with the reporter; in fact, when she presented her idea of writing a profile on their business, told her quite clearly that they weren't interested.

"It is circumstantial that Lisa Clark's body was found in an apartment building of over two hundred apartments. It is a fact that Mrs. Lorenza Rafkin and Aiden Rafkin have lived in the building since it first opened and have had no complaints filed about them by either the management or other tenants.

"At the current age of ninety-seven, Mrs. Rafkin can hardly be considered as a candidate for an accomplice, as presented by the DA. Furthermore, her grandson is and has always been seen by her side, so we cannot assume it is anything other than an example of a close family.

"Evidence of DNA found under Ms. Clark's fingernails has been proven inadmissible. Video camera coverage of the apartment building does not show either Mrs. Rafkin or Mr. Rafkin in the presence of Ms. Clark. We are therefore left with a cleverly built case of circumstantial evidence. Because you will be reviewing the elements of this case, I remind you that you must prove beyond reasonable doubt that Mr. and Mrs. Rafkin are guilty. Thank you for your service on this matter."

The people gathered in the audience immediately began whispering among themselves. If you judged the reaction by the comments overheard, you'd think they had already decided the guilt of the two people on trial for murder.

Susan remained in her seat, her head beginning to ache, trying to evaluate the effectiveness of the different summations. Frowning with fear that some of the jurors had found the evidence weak and might not vote guilty. Closing her eyes, she prayed for justice.

Chapter 33

Sonny Carola felt he'd been cut off from his boss. Did he do something wrong? No, that couldn't be. He'd been in the family doing this same job of transporting people from ships to drop-off at the local gas station for over twenty years. Yet, he needed help and didn't want to enrage Mrs. Rafkin by not getting her approval.

"Yes," he barked into his phone. He didn't need more worries. "Oh, sorry. Yes, I know you are calling for Mrs. Rafkin. Is she better? I understand she is being detained in a hospital?"

The voice on the phone was calm, but firm. Sonny knew it was a family representative, someone he'd met only once but had in the past year and a half spoken to on a regular basis. Since the *vecchia*, the old woman, had become ill, his orders were short, direct, and clearly meant to be followed.

"So we have an incoming tomorrow. Yes, but I must ask permission to hire help. My hip is really bad and I will need assistance with the boat."

Sonny nodded to the inquiry about whether or not he could vouch for the secrecy of this person and would he limit the job to simple transport from ship to boat and back to shore.

"Yea… yeah. Got it."

Bene. I can try out that guy at the bar. The decision was based solely on his ability to read people and his new acquaintance, Vic Rizzo, fit the bill… young, fit, and in need of money.

"It's a cash deal. You accompany me on my next run to pick up a guy, so you will know what to do the next time. My hip is making it difficult to handle a boat, rough seas, and transfers. If you can do some of my runs for me, we can add a bit to your pockets."

"Sounds easy enough. When do you want me to meet you and where?" Vic asked, delighted that his cover had been successful in gaining the old man's trust.

"Meet me here at the bar tomorrow at midnight. You'll travel with me and at the end, I'll bring you back to your car."

Nodding, Vic reached into his pocket and withdrew a money clip with twenties. "Hey, let me buy the next round to thank you. My wife will love the extra cash in her cookie jar."

Driving back to the city, Vic called Tom. "We're set. Tomorrow night I'll learn the answer to that all-consuming question of what the hell the Rafkins are up to. Sonny is hiring me to do the occasional job for him and tomorrow he'll take me on one of his runs. Where and what should be interesting," Vic said and clicked off. *Let's hope this old guy isn't armed or in better physical shape than he appears.*

* * *

163

Vic made sure he arrived five minutes before midnight to show his interest in the job. As Sonny strolled into the bar, he walked over and punched him on the shoulder, signaling he was to follow him out.

Waiting at the curb was a beat-up truck, one Vic had seen before. And it looked like the one Sam had described to Tom. Alert to any clues inside, he got in the passenger side as Sonny pulled out onto the narrow country road. This was always the part of an undercover operation that was tricky. It was a time when knowing nothing about what he'd face meant he had to be on full alert.

"Where are we going?" Vic asked in as casual a voice as possible, meanwhile watching the passing scenery for landmarks should he need to retrace the route in the future.

"I live in a house by the water. It's been home since I retired."

"You're kinda young to be retired." Vic's comment was meant to start a conversation.

Sonny looked at Vic with a broad smile showing a couple of crooked front teeth while nodding his approval. "Yup. Now I do pickup jobs for my friends. And, I like to fish. It runs in the family. This was my uncle's fishing shack."

They pulled up alongside a house that was more like a shack, and getting out of the truck, Vic wondered how long it had been standing. Its weathered wooden exterior was probably matched with a bare-bones interior. But looking at Sonny, thought it fit.

"OK, follow me," Sonny said and led Vic around to the water's edge of Long Island Sound. The water was calm and the buildings on either side of the shore were dark. At the end of a short dock sat a vintage wooden rowboat fitted out with an outboard motor, oars, and a covered locker. As Sonny took the helm, he pointed to the bow, indicating that was where Vic should sit.

"Hey, untie us." Following the old man's order, Vic stepped into the boat.

The motor purred, a sound of a well-maintained engine, thought Vic. Pulling away from the shore, Sonny slowly headed out to the main channel and, turning east, followed the shoreline but kept it at a distance.

"We're going to meet a fishing boat. Pick someone up and return. Easy way to make a hundred bucks and let me rest my bad hip," Sonny remarked. When Vic turned around, Sonny quickly added, "Of course, if you work out, they could be real money in it."

"Real money? I would love to have another solid gig to add to the one I have. Maybe I could retire early too?" *Will he take the bait?*

Sonny Carola smiled. *He's a hungry one. Bene.*

The night was dark with the moon in its last quarter, the seas calm, and the magic of stars studding the sky temporarily captured Vic's attention. When the boat lurched, he looked up and saw that Sonny had thrown a line to a trawler and was being secured alongside the larger craft. He couldn't hear what transpired between Sonny and the rough-looking seaman, but shortly after another man dressed in sailor's blues appeared on deck and, stepping over the side of the trawler, climbed down a rope ladder, landing softly on the rowboat. With a wool cap covering his head and a short, closely cut beard, it was hard to discern his features.

Vic was about to say something when he caught Sonny's steely eyed stare, quickly silencing him. In fact, no one spoke the entire hour trip back to the shore. For a minute, Vic thought he was safe with the passenger and Sonny looking elsewhere. Reaching into his pocket for his cell, he hoped to find a split second to snap a shot of both men.

When the boat was once again secured to the float, Sonny led both men to his truck and drove to a nearby gas station, parked, and walked over to a waiting car. Signaling the stranger over, Vic watched the man say something to Sonny and get into the car, which promptly drove away.

Sonny turned to Vic, handing him another hundred-dollar bill. "You interested in an occasional trip?"

"Yes. Call this number when you want me to fill in for you." Vic scribbled a phone number on a scrap of paper he had in his jacket pocket.

"OK then. I'll take you back to your car."

* * *

"People smuggling?" said Jace, who was once again at the local bar with Tom, reviewing their respective cases. "Was your guy able to get a photo of this stranger?"

"No, but Sam was shadowing Vic, and waited at the gas station, figuring that was where he would wait to be picked up and driven into New York. Sam was able to ID the guy as an international criminal into drugs and guns. He must have paid the Rafkins a hefty fee to be smuggled into the country. And if you count Al junior's forgery skills, this isn't your normal family."

"No, they just updated Daddy's rackets," Jace concluded.

"Unfortunately, the Rafkins are on trial and the case is going to the jury. Without your proof, I can't add charges to their case," said an extremely disappointed Jace.

"No, but they could be charged again with federal crimes after they've been put away for murder and forgery," Tom added.

"If we even suggest that the Rafkins are into this racket, we ruin your undercover operation. So, no, I won't add to the already serious charges of murder. I'm just praying that if convicted, the family doesn't appeal, and are released to await another day in court."

Jace sat silently before picking up his beer. Slamming the glass on the table, he looked like he was ready to kill someone. "This means that Sally is still in danger. Damn it! So far, she's obeyed my instructions to stop researching that book on money laundering."

"You have to remove yourself from that lie that you are only protecting her. If you stay away, maybe the Rafkins group will forget about her. Apparently, being incarcerated hasn't stopped their operations," Tom concluded regretfully.

"I'll get on to that tonight," Jace said, secretly praying that Sally listened.

Chapter 34

"The prosecution stated its case and the jury was sequestered until they come to a decision," Susan reported as Sally finished tossing a salad for their dinner.

"You look as though there weren't any surprises," Sally replied.

"No surprises, aside from the primary source of DNA being tampered with."

"Even so, you said that the DA's summation was thorough and the jury had paid attention. So is it you that seems to be in flux?" Sally asked, looking up from the salad bowl, studying her friend. She suspected Susan was feeling that her analysis of the day's courtroom revelations might be flawed.

"I worry that George Randall didn't do all he could in presenting the case. But damn it. Those thugs can't go free," Susan cried out.

"We're in the homestretch. Can't be defeatist now," Sally replied.

"We'll see tomorrow. But aside from one of the DNA samples being thrown out, the secondary DNA source linked the grandson to Lisa's bodily fluids found on the old woman's apartment rug. I was impressed by George's presentation of

Lisa's character and portfolio of positive articles. I particularly liked his comment that he wished all investigative reporters took the high road when doing their research. And that too many featured the sensationalism of a story, rather than the humanity of the people being profiled."

"And yet you have reservations," Sally said.

"It's that old woman. I'm sure she's faking. She's too mean and controlling to just sit in the courtroom day after day, like a meek little mouse stirring up sympathy by slumping down in her wheelchair."

"What makes you think she's faking? She is ninety-seven! When she took the stand, how did George treat her?"

"Oh, he was a master of diplomacy, afraid if he was too harsh it wouldn't go over well with the jury. Mrs. Rafkin's manner and dress suggest Lady, when you and I suspect she is a ruthless killer." Having spat that out in anger, Susan crossed herself.

"When the jury comes in, I am going to be in the courtroom. It's over and I haven't been called as a witness, so it must be safe. We can hear the verdict together," Sally said, and dished up the salad. Taking a sip of her wine, she recognized that it had been a stressful week for Susan.

* * *

The jury returned to the courtroom and Susan and Sally, seated in the last row, waited for the judge to read the verdict before the jury foreman read it aloud to the packed courtroom.

Susan poked Sally, getting her attention. "Do you see that man in the short-sleeved shirt wearing sunglasses in the last row on the other side of the courtroom?"

"Is he the one you said was here every day of the trial?" Sally asked.

"Yes. Jace said he was one of his."

"All rise," called the bailiff, and the room responded as the judge entered the room. Susan searched the jurors, trying to read expressions that would tell her how they voted. "*Psst,* Sally. Can you see anything in the jurors' faces?"

Shaking her head no, Sally shrugged and clasped her friend's hand. "We'll know in a minute."

"Will the jury please read the verdict." The judge's tone was all business.

The jury foreman rose. "We find Aiden Rafkin guilty of murder in the first degree. We find Lorenza Rafkin guilty by association."

She couldn't help it, but Susan applauded along with half of the courtroom. Sally smiled but remained still. This wasn't over. They both wanted the death penalty for Aiden, and life in prison for his grandmother.

The judge pounded his gavel for order. "We will reconvene next week for sentencing."

The room rose as one and the officers escorted Aiden out of the room in handcuffs, while a female officer wheeled Mrs. Rafkin out and back to medical lockup. "Did you see those two?" Susan whispered to Sally. "Not a hint of emotion. No scowl, pounding of the table. Nothing."

"It's in their eyes. Vengeance," Sally added and shivered.

* * *

Back at her apartment, Sally poured Susan and herself a large glass of wine. Hoisting it with a smile, she said, "Here's to justice."

As she set her glass down, her cell rang. "Sally, it's Jace. I heard you were in the courtroom. It's over. Are you alright?"

"Absolutely. We both are," Sally replied.

Jace began chuckling. "I knew you couldn't keep away. And I heard the verdicts. Susan must be pleased."

"Yes. And you don't have to remind us not to start working on our project. At least until Tom says we can."

"Say hi to Susan and thank her for copying me on her notes. You two are really observant, a gift not given to many these days," Jace said, relieved that they were obeying orders.

Chapter 35

It was the day they had been waiting for. A day of justice for Lisa Clark. The courtroom was filled with press. Apparently, the 1920s Mob still sold lots of papers.

Sally and Susan sat in the last row, fingers crossed, hoping the two odious Rafkins would never see freedom to rob or harm anyone ever again. They rose along with the rest in the courtroom as the judge entered.

The judge, now seated, cleared his throat. "Ladies and gentlemen, in the case of Aiden Rafkin, I sentence him to twenty years in a high-security prison with no opportunity of parole."

"He deserves life in prison," an agitated Susan whispered to Sally. "I'd give him the death penalty!"

The courtroom buzzed with people sharing their opinions of Aiden Rafkin's sentence. Susan and Sally held their breath. Their question the same, would Mrs. Rafkin get a reduced but equally well-deserved sentence? "Here we go," Susan whispered as Sally took firm hold of her hand.

When the courtroom quieted, the judge continued. "In the case of Mrs. Lorenza Rafkin, recognizing her state of health, I sentence her to five years in prison, less the one and a half already served, and the rest of her life under house arrest."

"What?" Susan almost shouted.

"If you think about it, the witch will be a hundred before she's released to house arrest. By that time, what harm can she do?" Sally asked, disappointed but trying to calm her friend.

"I don't trust the bitch to die before she's released. She has money to buy whatever she needs in prison, and people to handle her affairs. That, along with her hate, would probably fuel her for another decade," Susan snapped.

* * *

"Tom, Sally and Susan think this is over and they are safe," Jace explained. "I fully expect to be told they are back researching that book!"

Tom and Jace were back at the bar, glad that the murderers got their due. But Jace took a sip of celebratory scotch and began turning his glass around on the table.

"I think we have to let Sally and Susan listen to that audio tape. Just in case they unknowingly dig up or hear something we missed. Also, they need to know that prison hasn't shut down the Rafkin's Bayville enterprise," Tom said.

"You've read my mind. I'll bring them by tomorrow at ten."

* * *

Promptly at ten the next morning, Jace arrived with Sally and Susan, clearly in a more relaxed frame of mind. Now that the Rafkins were in jail, they told Jace that they would be getting back to their research.

Just what I was afraid of, he thought.

"Ladies, welcome once again to the FBI. If you will follow me," Tom said, ushering them to a smaller room than the one they met in before, with Jace following close behind. Once seated, Tom placed a tape recorder on the table. "I believe this is what you wanted to hear," he said and turned on the small black device.

My name is Carmine Gambino. I am the brother of Alfonse Gambino, and uncle to Lorenza. I am recording this document to leave behind a record of my life spent entirely in the service of my brother. I leave this and my life's savings to my nephew Sonny Carola, the only other blood family I have. Along with a bequest of $100,000 are instructions to take the remaining cash in the account to Sicily and give it to my mother's family.

When Alfonse was to marry Maria, it was me who brought her over from Sicily. I was fifteen and already a made man, having killed a cop trying to arrest one of Alfonse's runners collecting a monthly payment from a local grocer.

When Lorenza was born, I was entrusted with protecting both the little girl and her mother. When Maria died, Lorenza was six and it was me who took her to school and picked her up, and watched over her as she did her homework in her father's office. She was a smart one and slowly began to keep her father's books. Later, he entrusted her with parts of his various businesses.

The money was good and Alfonse had me travel to Cuba in the '30s with him and watch over Lorenza, while he opened a bank account and deposited a trunk full of cash. Every four months, I would take Lorenza and a set of luggage back to Cuba to add to their bank account.

Finally, Lorenza married at sixteen and bore a son she named Alfonse after her father. Her husband was an Irish cop on Alfonse's payroll, therefore considered worthy of his princess. When he died three years later, she changed her name from Rafferty to Rafkin and opened the bookshop. By that time, her father was passing along almost all of his business operations and soldiers to Lorenza's control. My responsibility was switched from her to protecting her young son.

I am recording these notes as a testament to having lived my life with honor, as a trusted member of my brother's family and overseer of his daughter and her business interests.

This recording, along with my will containing instructions to have my story published, are being left with my lawyer. It is my wish for those who thought me a no-account weakling, to know I was entrusted with the life and interests of Alfonso's jewel, his princess.

When the tape stopped, all sat quietly lost in their own thoughts.

"Ladies, if you have any thoughts to add to this information, I'd appreciate hearing them," Tom said.

"That leaves me with more questions than answers," Sally said, watching Tom remove the tape from the recorder and replace it in the envelope with Lisa's notes. "Lisa couldn't have gotten this information from this man; he'd be one hundred and twelve by now."

"I need to think on this," Susan said. "My question is that after ninety-plus years, where is that money now? And you're right, how did Lisa get this information?"

"Back to basics. If this man took trunks full of cash to Cuba before Castro, they must have moved it again in the late '50s to protect it from Castro's revolutionary government," Sally surmised.

"Where is Carmine's nephew? Is he the man Lisa met?" Susan asked.

Tom held up one hand to stop both women from their very astute questions. He now had an idea of the pressure Jace was under, trying to keep them safe from their own actions.

"If I may, Mrs. Clark, we haven't found any evidence of money laundering. And a check with Mr. Gambino's attorney discovered that he had given this information to Lisa, with the understanding that she would publish a truthful article that showed his client in a good light."

"So we can use this information in our book?" she asked.

"Not yet. Unless you limit it to the Rafkin family matriarch, and not the as-yet-to-prove source of their fortune." Tom was the FBI agent in charge and his word on the matter final.

"The fortune. Follow the money. We believe that Lorenza's father left her a fortune that in today's dollars would be worth billions. Just because he kept shifting the location of his offshore banks to keep it secret, doesn't mean she hasn't continued to stash illegal profits in a similar fashion," Sally stated. Looking around, she spotted a coffee urn. "Susan, coffee?" Getting approval, she got up and poured two cups, returned to the table, and gave her full attention back to Tom. "Sorry. I'm addicted," she said sweetly.

Jace, watching her act, wasn't fooled, wondering what she'd ask next.

Tom looked to Jace and saw that this woman wouldn't leave the money laundering aspect of the case alone. Taking a chair opposite Sally, Tom cleared his throat. "Mrs. Scott, what I am about to share with you must not leave this room. It addresses your comment: follow the money," Tom began and then turned his attention to Susan. "This applies to you as well, Mrs. Clark."

Receiving assurances from both women that nothing would leave the room, he crossed his fingers. "We are currently involved in an undercover operation that so far has enabled the FBI to penetrate the people-smuggling operation run by the Rafkins. However, our agent has only just been accepted as a hired hand and taken a short boat ride to pick up a man from a fishing trawler. Without knowing where he came from, or his final destination, there is nothing we can do but wait."

With the ringing of Tom's cell, he excused himself and left the room. It wasn't long before a very angry man returned. "I was just alerted that the man under surveillance, the one we believe was smuggling people into this country, has died. The trail ends with him."

"Natural causes?" Jace asked.

"An autopsy wasn't done. The man collapsed in a bar, and by the time the EMS arrived, he had died. They took him to the morgue, where a lawyer turned up with papers to have the body cremated. And the local police, not thinking anything untoward about a seventy-year-old local fisherman in poor health dying, released the body."

Epilogue

"Have either you, Mrs. Clark or Mrs. Scott, ever been on television?" asked Frances Delroy, host of the PBS program *Meet the Author.*

"No, neither of us has," responded Susan Clark with a nod to Sally. "Ms. Delroy, please call us by our first names."

"And please do the same," Frances Delroy replied with a smile. "Well, this isn't a Broadway production, simply a table around which our viewers can meet the authors of this amazing book. Relax and if I ask a question you don't feel comfortable in answering, simply lift a hand and I'll change direction. Alright?" Frances asked in the charming soft voice that was a hallmark of her success as a television host. A former crime reporter, she was fascinated by these two normal women, wondering how they could write a chilling biography on such a dangerous family.

Sally was happy that the studio did not have an audience. The crew for lighting, camera, and teleprompter seemed intent on making them comfortable. No one said a harsh word to them during the preshow meeting. Instead, each crew member took time to introduce themselves and give a brief description of their job and where they would be standing. By the time the meeting was over, Sally was glad Susan's publishing company made this their first of many interviews. The publicist had explained that it would give them experience in guiding an interviewer's questions. They didn't have to answer anything that made them uncomfortable, but could instead give an acceptable alternative reply.

Susan had suggested that they dress in simple suits to show a professional approach to their work. When she caught herself on the monitor off to one side of the set, Sally had to admit that her navy jacket, white shell of a blouse, and tailored black pants photographed well.

Settled around a small round table with a glass of water next to each participant, the floor director began his countdown. "Five, four, three, two, one." At which point the camera light went green.

"Today is one of the most interesting interviews I've hosted in a long time. My guests are Susan Clark and Sally Scott, coauthors of *Follow the Money*, a book that, while depicting a real-life story of one family, reads like a thriller. And to their credit, it is their first book."

Sally, watching a video screen, saw the camera move from the host to each of them. Susan looking younger than her sixty-seven years.

"Today's guests should give hope to anyone who ever thought they might want to write a book. Mrs. Clark had a career as an executive assistant, and Mrs. Scott has an accounting practice. Neither has ever attempted to write a book before."

"Susan, let me start with you. I understand this book was written to honor your niece Lisa Clark. Would you please explain to our viewers." Before answering, Susan turned to Sally for support.

"Yes, Frances. My niece Lisa Clark was an investigative journalist researching the background activities of one family. Four years ago, she was murdered to keep her quiet. Before she died, all she told me was the research would be for an exposé about money laundering, and saying anything more would place me in danger."

"Sally, how did you and Susan become acquainted?" Frances asked with her focus now on Sally.

"Unfortunately, I was the one to spot Lisa's body in the elevator of our apartment building. Susan and I are neighbors. During the investigation, we became friends, sharing theories about who had killed her niece. When she asked me to help her finish Lisa's book, I agreed. I felt a personal connection to the young woman and wanted to help complete the book that cost her life."

"Susan, your book, *Follow the Money*, discloses the criminal activities of one family going back almost a century. Will you tell us more about this family?" Frances asked, leaning forward, not wanting to miss a word.

"The book follows the Rafkin family, primarily Lorenza Rafkin, daughter of a 1920s mobster, Alfonse Gambino. As his only child, she was raised in his business of liquor smuggling, extortion, gambling, speakeasies, and prostitution."

"Just how profitable were those illicit businesses?"

"Alfonso was a cousin of Carlo Gambino, who was head of the Five Families that ruled New York during prohibition. Due to his loyalty, Carlo deeded Alfonso a small portion of his empire. That piece of his business was pulling in an estimated three million a week."

"Sally, as an accountant, can you tell us what that would be in today's dollars?"

"More than forty billion." Frances, straightening up and looking into the camera, whispered, "Wow."

Susan, fearing that the host would dig more deeply into the Rafkins' activities, quickly continued her explanation. "Frances, money laundering was the only thing my niece said she was researching. I am not sure she knew just how much was involved, just that it was sizable."

"Money laundering?" Frances asked.

"Yes, a term that came into use when the Mob-owned laundromats exchanged dirty money and replaced it as legitimate earnings. With the government instituting income tax, they needed some way to account for their profits." Susan was pleased to see Frances nod with understanding.

"In the book, you tell of the family's money management practices and that they complied with the current tax law. But you also say they had a hidden source of income. What did they do with that?" Frances asked.

"We found an investment bank, with subsidiaries that appear on the Rafkins' financial records. Allied Investments, an investment bank based in Malta, has Lorenza Rafkin on its board. As such she receives legitimate income from the firm's profits. Additionally, the Rafkins rent their apartments from Allied Realty, a subsidiary. All transactions are reported as required by our financial laws," Susan explained.

"As an accountant, I was curious as to where the current family kept or hid the wealth bequeathed to them by Mrs. Rafkin's father, and what they did with their illegal earnings today," Sally said, and watched Frances's attention shift to her. "If you read further, you will see that we only came up with legitimate earnings."

Frances continued, "In the book, you show how, as a small girl, she would move money from one offshore bank to another each time circumstances threatened to confiscate their savings. But you also write that this practice of hiding their wealth continued to the present."

"We have identified those early banks in Cuba and the Caymans. However, we have been unsuccessful in uncovering the location of Mrs. Rafkin's inherited wealth, or any income from possible illegal activities," Sally explained.

"In reading this extraordinary tale, you take readers back a century in the life of one family. It is almost as if you lived those years with them. Why was it important for you to describe life down through the years?"

"It isn't often that you find one person with an active life well into her nineties. Or that this person was head of a family and its various business enterprises. As a businesswoman myself, she intrigued me. And in looking into her past found that she was as canny as any financial executive today," Sally said.

"I'd like to add that offshore banking has become synonymous with criminal activities. But Malta, as the location of an investment bank, would not be on top of most people's lists," Frances said.

"Yes, Malta has a long history of wealth being transferred from abroad. The island was deeded to the Knights of St. John by Charles V in 1530. The priests, second sons of wealthy European families, governed the island, overseeing its economic, civic, and healthcare institutions, and building fortifications to keep it safe from a threatened invasion by Suliman's army," Sally began.

"But Malta? It isn't the first country I'd associate with wealth," Frances remarked.

"You have to understand their history. You see, the priests received all manner of wealth in gold, silver, jewels, and art gifted by their families. In addition to managing the country, the order built churches and embellished them with their donated treasure."

"Sally, I am sure our viewers would like to know how treasure in the sixteenth century relates to money today," Frances said.

"Let me bring you up to date then," Sally said with a smile. She loved this part of the story. "All went well until Napoleon invaded in 1798 and forced the priests to deed the island to him. The priests returned to their original role of hospitaller caring for the needs of the sick and poor, while appealing to Britain for help. Britain came to their aid and, in ousting Napoleon in 1800, restored law and order to the Maltese people. Throughout the following centuries, Malta became a profitable trading port and continued to add to the wealth of the church and its people. After World War II, it was a time of rebuilding from the extensive damage by German bombing runs, and along with the city infrastructure, was the establishment of firms, including Allied Investments. Our research leads us to think that during the war most of the island's wealth was hidden. Later it was transferred secretly to reestablish and launch new businesses that continue to this day," Sally explained and raised her hand to signal Frances to stop her line of questioning.

The silence that followed had Frances nod and rethink her following remarks. "Ladies and gentlemen, we will take a short break for a message from our station."

"Frances, if you continue to discuss possible hiding of the Rafkin wealth, you will be placing Susan and I in jeopardy." With the camera off and the balance of the interview still to come, Frances wasn't sure how to proceed.

Seeing the problem, Sally spoke up. "May I suggest that you ask Susan about the Rafkin trial. She was in the courtroom every day and maybe that can limit our exposure." Seeing the camera light once again turn green, all she could do was cross her fingers and hope that the host understood.

"Welcome back. I was just about to ask Susan about the trial that sent the Rafkins to prison."

"Frances, I'm sure you can understand why I wanted to be in that courtroom to make sure that the murderer and his grandmother received the maximum punishment for the death of my niece. And when the verdict came in, Aiden Rafkin was convicted of first-degree murder and sentenced to twenty years in jail without opportunity of parole." Susan's delivery was more forceful than her previous statements.

"And Mrs. Rafkin, what was her sentence? I would hate to be on that jury deciding the fate of a crippled ninety-seven-year-old woman who didn't look like she could care for herself, let alone assist her grandson in murdering a healthy young woman," Frances said.

"Difficult, but necessary. The jury said that they had taken her deteriorating health into consideration but found her guilty of assisting her grandson in Lisa's murder, having lured her to her apartment and providing drugs that were found in Lisa's system. Her verdict was five years in prison, less the year and a half for time served, followed by house arrest for the rest of her life."

"Ladies, I couldn't put your book down. I hope you have another book in your future," Frances said.

With Susan's laughter and shaking of her head, Frances knew she had accomplished her one goal—to publish her niece's book. "And for you, Sally?"

"I'm truly flattered, Frances. However, I have a full plate with my accounting practice and family responsibilities," Sally said with great delight. "This was a nerve-racking but thrilling one-time adventure."

"We're almost out of time; is there anything else you would like our viewers to know?"

Sally, with kindness in her heart, looked into the camera. "I would like to say that this case would not have been solved without the excellent work of the New York City detectives and their team of experts. Even though it took time to gather the evidence that would provide Lisa Clark the justice she so greatly deserved, they never gave up."

"I would like to add to Sally's praise for the detectives. I'd also like to leave your viewers with this thought. There may come a time when you are faced with a difficult situation. If Sally and I had stopped researching this family, it would haunt me to the end of my days. In completing my niece's book, I can let it go and move on with my life," Susan added.

The following momentary silence was due to Frances listening to her producer's voice in her earpiece. Holding up a copy of the book for the audience to see, she happily announced, "I just received word that *Follow the Money* is number one on *The New York Times* bestseller list."

Susan looked to Sally and wreathed in smiles, they shook hands.

Reaching across the table, Frances placed her hand on top of Susan's and Sally's, clasping them warmly. Then turned back to the camera. "Thank you, Susan Clark and Sally Scott, for sharing your author journey with us. It is a true-life thriller. And to all of you, start that book. This is Frances Delroy, saying Good Day."

The End

Author's Note

Reader loyalty has inspired me to complete this trilogy that follows a young woman through trying circumstances and eventually realizes that decisions and actions of the past were undertaken while blinded by first love, a widow's isolation, and distancing herself from those she loves.

When I sit down to pen a novel, I look for those blind spots that impact a woman's life. We all have them, and in some instances I include mine. The question is, will Sally Scott, now free of delusions of the past, be ready to move on and fly free to new adventures?

I look forward to hearing from you and your thoughts on Sally's next adventure. One way is for you to write a review and post it on Amazon. That way others—including myself—will benefit from your theories.

Thank you all, especially those who continue to read my novels and write a review for others to share.

Patricia E. Gitt

patriciagitt.com

Made in the USA
Middletown, DE
25 August 2023

37252102R00116